MANN OF THE MEDICAL WING

Maurice Mann, the serious young RMO at St. Mary's Hospital, found it more than a little embarrassing to have his irrepressible young sister Felicity as a student nurse in the same hospital. Her penchant for getting into trouble was a thorn in his side. When she asked him to meet her friend Bridget Moore off a train, he agreed, but unfortunately he met the wrong girl!

ANNE DURHAM

MANN OF THE MEDICAL WING

Complete and Unabridged

LINFORD
Leicester

Middle Georgia Regional Library
Macon, Georgia

First published in Great Britain in 1968 by
Mills and Boon Ltd.,
London

First Large Print Edition
published April 1986
by arrangement with
Mills and Boon Ltd.,
London

British Library CIP Data

Durham, Anne
    Mann of the medical wing.—Large print ed.—
Linford romance library
    Rn: Emily Kathleen Walker   I. Title
823'.914[F]   PR6073.A411/

ISBN 0-7089-6175-4

Published by
F. A. Thorpe (Publishing) Ltd.
Anstey, Leicestershire
Set by Rowland Phototypesetting Ltd.
Bury St. Edmunds, Suffolk
Printed and bound in Great Britain by
T. J. Press (Padstow) Ltd., Padstow, Cornwall

1

THE Medical Wing at St. Mary's had wards named after early benefactors of the hospital. It was old, and so were the names of the wards. In one of the women's wards—the Sibylla Stansfield Ward—three 'old-timers' were busy initiating a new patient into the mysteries of 'knowing the ropes'. In a medical ward, where the patients tend to stay longer than on the surgical wards, there are always those who like to take the newcomers under their wing.

Mrs. Mobbs was like that. An enormous woman, she had been in that corner bed for so long that she was almost an institution. "Glands, I got, dear," she told Mrs. Binny. "Starve me, that's what they do, but it don't make no difference. I tell 'em they'll have to have a special big bed made for me soon. What are you in for, dear?"

1

The usual opening gambit. Mrs. Binny said faintly, "I don't know yet. They're going to do tests."

"Ah, tests," Mrs. Mobbs said judicially. "I've seen that before. X-rays and barium meal and things. Is it your stomach, then —terrible pains here?" and she demonstrated.

Mrs. Binny looked apprehensive. "Not yet I haven't got pains there. It's my head. I have blackouts and sometimes I don't remember where I've been or what I've been doing."

Mrs. Mobbs was really interested now. She exchanged a significant look with Mrs. Hooker, who was on the far side of Mrs. Binny. Mrs. Hooker was so thin and sunken, the nurses declared they could lift her with one hand. "We've seen this before, haven't we, dear?"

Mrs. Hooker nodded sagely. "Real interesting, the last one was, wasn't it? Weren't they surprised, too, when they got the answer from those test-tubes?"

Mrs. Binny said fearfully, "What have I got, then?"

2

"Oh, we can't say, dear. You might not have the same thing. We're only saying that the symptoms started the same as you've got. Don't you worry, duck, they'll call in the path. boys on the job. A right lot they are over in the path. lab., eh, Mrs. H?"

"My, they are," Mrs. Hooker agreed. "But none of them as nice as Dr. Mann. He's my favourite."

"Mine, too," Mrs. Mobbs said. "He's gorgeous. If I was only ten years younger—"

"And not so fat," Mrs. Hooker couldn't resist adding. She was worried about her spare frame and got her pleasure from teasing her enormous neighbour.

Mrs. Binny said, "I think I'll write and tell my husband. I've never been away from him before," she faltered.

Mrs. Mobbs sized her up. She would be in her early thirties, Mrs. Mobbs decided. "Not a newly-wed, are you?" she asked.

"No, I've been married ten years."

"Then it'll do you both good to be apart for a bit, and I wouldn't get out all that writing stuff, if I were you. You won't get any peace for writing letters, not for ages yet."

"But surely all this coming and going will be over soon?" Mrs. Binny gasped in dismay. "Someone comes in and out every few minutes. I thought hospitals were quiet places."

That amused the other two very much. "Bless you, duck, it'll go on for a good many hours yet. Starting with five-thirty in the morning—"

"Five-thirty?" Mrs. Binny gasped. "Oh, I'm never awake at that hour. My John doesn't call me until half past nine when he's going to work."

"Then you'll be getting some new experiences, won't you, dear?" Mrs. Mobbs said with a fat chuckle. "Oh, I know some hospitals have gone a bit easier on the patients. The new hospitals don't wake you till six or even half past, but not St. Mary's. It's the night staff, you see. Short-handed, and they like to make a beginning betimes. So up you get for a scalding hot cuppa at five-thirty and then it's BP round and washings, and beds and medicines and temperatures and any special drugs."

"Drugs?" Mrs. Binny whispered.

"Oh, yes, dear, Number Seven has been out cold for weeks, and so has Number Ten. I wish sometimes I could be put to sleep, and wake up to find I was five stone lighter," and that set her and her friend laughing again.

"Then they start cleaning the ward," Mrs. Hooker put in, but Mrs. Mobbs was telling the story and said so.

"The day staff come on next, and the flowers are brought in. Oh, yes, they always take them out at night, dear, in case they get knocked over in the dark. Besides, they have to find a few extra jobs for the young nurses, keep them on the run, in case we forget to keep asking for things. And then it's breakfast."

"And then the night staff go off duty," Mrs. Hooker put in quickly, and unexpectedly a hollow voice on the other side of Mrs. Mobbs put in: "Then the Report's read."

"Oh, is that you awake, Mrs. Gadd?" Mrs. Mobbs shook her head and clicked her tongue. "Come up for air, she has," she told Mrs. Binny. "Sleeps her life away. They don't need to put her on drugs."

"What's the matter with her?" Mrs. Binny asked fearfully.

"Gastric. Don't talk to her about food, whatever you do. It drives her wild. All she craves for is a nice plate of fish and chips—"

"With vinegar," Mrs. Gadd moaned, and went to sleep again.

"Then it's ward prayers," Mrs. Mobbs took up the story, "and the medicines what we have to have after breakfast, then Sister does her round."

"And then the ward door bangs a few more times when the nurses go off to coffee or to change their aprons," Mrs. Hooker nipped in.

"Then the special treatments trolleys come in, and the wheels clang and squeak," Mrs. Mobbs continued. "And I forgot to mention that housemen and students are popping in and out all the time, though they're not supposed to—"

"And the doors open to medical staff between nine-thirty and twelve," Mrs. Hooker put in triumphantly.

"You forgot the newspaper woman's round," Mrs. Mobbs reproached her, "to say nothing of the library lady and the shop trolley and the clergy—all five of them," she said, with delight, as she twisted to look into the dismayed face of Mrs. Binny. "And in between all that, someone'll come and pull the curtains round you, and strip you down, and all the students will crowd round and ask silly questions."

"In some hospitals," Mrs. Hooker put in, "they give you a mask to put on, so you won't be embarrassed."

"I'd be dead of shame. A mask wouldn't help me," Mrs. Binny declared, her lips wobbling and her eyes filling. "Besides, why would they want to strip me naked when it's my head that's bothering me?"

"Routine, dear. Hospitals are always run on routine. They strip you naked and thump you all over even if it's a big toe ache you've got."

After a pause, Mrs. Binny said, "Well, when *can* I write to my husband?"

Mrs. Gadd woke up to say, "Don't listen to them, dear. Just keep your pad and pencil handy and whip it out every time they leave you alone. If you don't snatch the spare minutes, it won't get you anywhere. But look sharp for when they come and strip your bed, 'cos everything goes flying. Especially if you keep a hankie under the pillow. I lost a lot that way!"

"Aren't the nurses any good, then?" Mrs. Binny gasped.

"Oh, now, I didn't say that, now did I? Overworked if you like, but they're not a bad lot, not the ones we've got at the moment."

"Do they change them, then?"

"Oh, yes, dear, with a thing called General post. It's supposed to be every three months, but it seems to me they swap 'em round when they like. Just when you get used to a little nurse, then she's gone, and you hear she's been put on the children's ward or sent down to Casualty or something with no sense to it."

"Well, look what we've got today, then," Mrs. Mobbs broke in, impatient to take the stage again. "How about that, then?"

Mrs. Binny looked at the door. Two young nurses were backing in with the trolley of special drinks, and another, who was supposed to be helping, stood holding the door and allowing her glance to stray round, a half smile playing about her lips. For sheer loveliness, this girl was streets ahead of anything Mrs. Binny had seen. Dreamy gentleness, eyes incredibly blue, and hair the colour of warm ripening corn, and she wore a distinctive uniform like a nylon overall with a little cap to match, of a shade of lilac infinitely becoming to her.

"Do they have hairdressers here, then?" Mrs. Binny couldn't believe it.

That made the other women laugh and the girl looked across at them. Mrs. Mobbs signalled to her and she willingly deserted the others, letting the door go with a slam. "Look out!" Mrs. Mobbs cried, but it was too late. It smacked one of the juniors on the bottom and the trolley whizzed down the ward, catching the staff nurse in the midriff.

"Nurse Mann!" she said wearily. "It's you again, is it?"

"Yes, Staff, sorry, Staff," the lovely girl said, but she couldn't keep her face straight, and soon she had even the staff nurse unwillingly smiling. "Do be careful, for heaven's sake," she begged, going off briskly and leaving them to it.

"Mann, you stupid thing—" one of the juniors said wrathfully, and the other said, "Felicity, you take the biscuit. How do you expect to get through PTS?"

"I don't, darling," the golden girl said ruefully, and went over to Mrs. Mobbs. "Nearly came to grief then," she said, and rolled up into gales of giggles.

"You silly giggly thing, you—they never smacked your bottom enough when you were a kiddie," Mrs. Mobbs scolded. "Mrs. Binny here thinks you're a hairdresser—how about that?"

That set the girl off laughing again.

"Oh, don't, darling—don't make me laugh. Besides, I have to hurry—tell me this. Has my beloved brother been round yet? No? Good show, because d'you see, I've asked him to do something for me."

"Not again!" Mrs. Mobbs begged.

"Yes, and after last time's disaster he might just refuse, but as it's to meet a friend of mine off the train, if I keep out of his sight he won't be able to do anything else but get the car and go. See, darlings? I must fly."

"Just a minute, love—what's wrong with a taxi for your pal?"

"She's as scatty as I am—she won't know where to tell them to drop her. Actually I'm pretty sure I'm the only one who won't get through the exams next week, so I thought if I've got to go through PTS all over again, it might be fun to have my own friend with me instead of a lot of new bods. 'Bye!"

She skidded down the ward and out of the other end, without doing a thing to help.

"How about that?" Mrs. Mobbs said to

the others. And because Mrs. Binny was still hoping she was a hairdresser in that lilac overall Mrs. Mobbs explained. "PTS uniform, dear—preliminary training school. They come over on the wards once a week for an hour or two, to get the feel of it. Me, I'm scared she'll make a mistake when the drinks are coming to me. She could do a real mischief, that one."

"Why do they let her stay, then?" Mrs. Binny asked anxiously.

"Only because she's Dr. Mann's young sister, you can bet your sweet life! Anyone else would have been kicked out long ago if they'd been as daft as she is—or pretends to be. Me, I think she's determined to go through life larking about, so she won't get the dirty jobs to do, and I can't say I blame her. These young girls are no better than waitresses and charwomen, to my way of thinking. And the hours they're on their poor feet! I wouldn't let any girl of mine be a nurse."

"I would," Mrs. Gadd broke in, "if I had a girl, that is, which I haven't. I reckon it's a nice life. Well, always something different going on, different faces, living and eating together, all them young doctors about, and the fun they have with their socials and their tennis and swimming and I don't know what."

"Well, whichever way it is, we're going to have two of 'em, two scatty ones and not just one! Oh, and her brother's such a dear feller, you wouldn't believe. If I was to tell you, Mrs. Binny, that that man is about the only shy young man I know, you wouldn't believe me. Oh, look out, here he comes!"

He was a very tall young man, and his hair wasn't golden like his sister's, but a darkish brown. But he had blue eyes like hers, and the same straight nose and determined chin. There, however, the resemblance ended. Mrs. Binny felt better, for a start. If that young man was one of the doctors here, then it wouldn't be so bad. He had a look about him that made her feel straight away that she could trust him with her life. And when he began to go round the beds, she was enthralled to find that he appeared to be completely interested in the one person, an unhurried little examination, not all raring to get on to the next patient, like some of the overworked staff she had already seen.

The staff nurse came over and stood beside him, lifting the charts from the end of the bed, and answering his questions. Mrs. Mobbs thought this was a pity, because she couldn't very well tell him in front of the staff nurse that his sister had been on the ward and had narrowly avoided the trouble again. Besides, it was rumoured that the staff nurse was sweet on Dr. Mann, and that was probably why, at the moment, she was going very easily with the way she treated that young sister of his. Even Mrs. Mobbs, who found Felicity a sheer joy in an otherwise rather dull middle-aged world, had to admit that to work with her must have been punishment indeed.

Dr. Mann wasn't unaware of the way the women looked at him. He had seen his sister come over from the PTS, but he hadn't been sharp enough to catch her.

When he had finished his round, he telephoned down to the switchboard to catch Felicity as she went out. With a bit of luck the head porter would look round and find her when he went for his cup of tea. He was a good sort.

Somehow, someone found Felicity before Dr. Mann had finished in the next ward. He went to the telephone gladly, confident that he could get rid of this tiresome errand she wanted to send him on.

Felicity said at once, "Maurice darling, I'm being a pig worrying you like this, aren't I, but it is rather special really."

"How special?" he asked guardedly.

"Darling, I can't exactly tell you over the phone. It's personal and private, or else I could have asked one of the ambulances to pick her up."

"Felicity, have you gone mad?" he stuttered. "You can't do that."

"Why not? I thought our ambulance drivers were perfectly respectable. Aren't they?"

"That isn't the point. You just can't do that. Understand, you can neither have your friends given lifts in ambulances, nor can you go joy-riding in them."

"Joy-riding in an ambulance? Why didn't I think of that?" she said innocently. "Oh, well, no, perhaps not. Don't flap, Maurice darling. The thing is, I know you go over to Latchmarket sometimes, so I thought you might be a dear and just pick Bridget up off the four o'clock train."

"But that's the whole point, Felicity— I don't even know what she looks like. Why can't you take a cab and meet your friend?"

"Because I'm not allowed out for a week," she admitted dolefully.

"Oh, no, not more trouble," he said faintly. "What is it this time?"

"Also too personal and private to say over the phone, but darling Maurice, I promise you I didn't mean to do such a thing to the beastly dummy."

"What, the dummy in the PTS that you all practise on?"

"Yes, *please* don't ask what I did to it —Sister Tutor wasn't at all pleased. She just didn't find it funny. So you see, you really must help me out just this once. And, darling Maurice, of course you can recognise my friend Bridget—she's got my case. The one you slashed by a mistake and the scar is still there after the mender man tried to stitch it up. Golly, I just thought—he'd be no good in the operating theatre, would he?"

"Felicity, stop laughing and tell me what she looks like," he said sharply.

"What? Oh, I can't describe people, darling. I'm no good at it. You know that. She's just a girl. The first girl you see, if she's lugging my case you maltreated, that'll be her. I must go, darling, and I do thank you from the bottom of my heart for helping out like this. You ought to be grateful to her—she'll probably have a steadying influence on me."

She put the receiver down hastily, so that her brother shouldn't hear her collapsing with laughter at the idea of her best friend Bridget Moore being a steadying influence on anyone. Probably they would both be thrown out in a week, once Bridget had settled in. She had been the despair of the staff at school. Sister Tutor wouldn't care for poor Bridget at all.

Just as Maurice Mann was leaving the hospital later that afternoon, he was called back to Casualty for an emergency, and had to admit the badly hurt person from an accident in Uxley Green's High Street. There had been an old property in course of demolition to make way for the new department-store, and part of a wall had collapsed and fallen beyond the barriers. Some of the injured had been taken into Wilmington. This man had been brought to St. Mary's. Maurice was kept some time, and when he did get away, he had to move himself, to get to Latchmarket in time to meet the London train.

It was a hectic journey. Uxley Green had no semblance left of the village its name suggested. It was now a town, a town without planning, with very little to recommend it at all except the rather nice reaches of the river outside the town. But beyond it, between Uxley Green and Latchmarket, was a little countryside left.

The last few farms after the builders and planners had erected little monotonous new towns; scanty patches of woodland where new houses were already encroaching; a swampy low-lying mess where the three rivers met, but which was always a virulent green, and sprinkled with lush willows. Not the lovely country that Dr. Mann's home was situated in.

Home, and the need to go back there, was not a thought he wanted to intrude at the moment. Felicity should be there, and not here to worry him. But the grandparents couldn't cope with her, and naturally thought that as he was on the hospital staff he would be able to keep an eye on her. Hospitals had, in their day, been places of sharp and efficacious discipline. Not so now, he thought dismally, as he recalled the nonsense from Felicity and her friends that Sister Tutor put up with, and the licence taken with time, which Home Sister closed a tired eye to.

This new friend of Felicity's, what on earth would she be like? And supposing that Felicity and she romped through another twelve weeks in PTS and still they weren't thrown out? How long would they be allowed to stay there, wasting everyone's time, just because Felicity happened to be the sister of one of the medical staff? He had no real illusions as to why she was being kept on, although of course Sister Tutor and Home Sister were probably praying that one day Felicity would conform sufficiently to be pushed over to the hospital, there to have the nonsense knocked out of her with a succession of washing the sluices and bath-rooms out, mac-scrubbing and other chastening chores that had dampened the enthusiasm and the misplaced energy of a lot of eighteen-year-olds.

But what if Felicity didn't ever manage to become a nurse, even a very indifferent one? Heaven knew that another pair of hands was needed, even for those lowly tasks, but supposing—just supposing—she tried authority too far and they invited her to leave? What was he going to do with her? He couldn't send her back to the grandparents. It wasn't fair. He supposed wearily that the grandparents would gently suggest that he should find a husband for Felicity. Perhaps indeed that had been at the back of their innocent old minds: hospital—doctors—pretty girl—plenty of choice of a future husband, a safe husband. His grandfather was fond of saying that doctors were people no one could do without. A safe profession. Fine for young ladies nowadays.

Except that Felicity wasn't a young lady but an attractive, even lovable hoyden, and Maurice flinched from the thought of somehow inflicting her on one of the younger men in his profession for life!

He reached the station in good time after all. He had been lucky with the traffic lights, but fussed somehow, because meeting someone he didn't know was not a thing he cared about doing.

He took out his sister's note again and studied it. Bridget Moore would be carrying his sister's old suitcase, and that was about the only coherent thing his sister had offered by way of description. No indication as to whether this Bridget would be dark, fair, a brunette or a redhead; tall or short, fat or thin, good-looking or hopelessly plain. He hoped devoutly that the girl wouldn't be dressed in the height of fashion, that somewhat deplorable fashion Felicity cared so much about, and he also hoped that she wouldn't be flirty, loud-voiced or giggly. He couldn't really say he had ever liked one of his sister's friends.

He remembered with sharp dismay that he hadn't asked Felicity who or what this Bridget Moore expected to be meeting her. Felicity had most likely mentioned her brother on the off chance of persuading him to be the reception party. In fact, she had probably sent a photograph of him. It would be like her to do something like that. With such an alarming thought in mind, he decided to stand just behind one of the slot machines, so that he could see and not be seen. And then the train came in.

It was a very crowded train, a corridor train, and he had no notion of where the girl would alight. He tried to look everywhere at once, but almost everyone had gone before he noticed the girl in brown. In a quiet sort of way she was the most elegant young woman he had seen for a long time. Her eyes were brown, and her hair such a dark brown it was almost but not quite black, and the only relief in the all-brown note was an elegant scarf knotted round her throat, a brown silk scarf with a muted pattern in yellows, oranges and grey. She stood thinking, a small girl given height by very high heels, but she was carrying the case—the slashed case he had been told to look out for.

He went forward confidently. This wasn't going to be so bad, he thought. Fancy Felicity, of all people, having such a nice friend!

Then a crowd of last-minute young people pelted off the train, just behind the girl, swarming all round her, laughing and talking, almost cutting her off from his view. They rushed past, shouting ineffectively for a porter, and as they did so, the girl—her face now sheet-white—slid to the ground and lay crumpled, the case on the ground beside her.

The young people came swarming back, and a porter came with them. People waiting on the other platform came across, and as he knelt down by her side, he found himself hemmed in, surrounded.

Like most shy men, once on his own job, he forgot his own diffidence and found an air of authority. "It's all right, I'm a doctor. Stand back there, please, and let her have some air."

A policeman materialised, and Maurice explained, "It's a friend of my sister's—I came to meet her." The policeman cleared a way for him to carry the girl to the waiting-room and someone carried the case. A woman from the canteen brought a cup of tea. The crowd melted away as the other train came in, and the girl opened her eyes.

"Take it easy," Maurice said bracingly. Just as he might have spoken to Felicity; firmly, encouragingly, for after all, these young student nurses were, for the most part, no more than eighteen. His ten years' seniority made him feel suddenly old and serious and a little behind the times.

The girl regarded him gravely. "I feel ill," she said quietly. "What happened to me?"

She had a very nice voice; soft, clear diction. How was it Felicity had thought that this girl would be the one to romp through PTS with, for heaven's sake?

"I'm afraid you fainted, Miss Moore," he told her. "Do you feel you can sit up and drink this? My car is outside the station, but we'll have you in hospital in no time at all."

"In hospital?" she said sharply. "But surely there's no need for that?" She sat with her head in her hands, waiting for him to answer.

"Didn't you realise you'd be living next door to the hospital?" he asked in an amused voice. "The Nurses' Home is only just across the grounds. My sister should have come to meet you herself, but she couldn't get away. I expect you'll guess why."

He waited for her to say something

about Felicity's perpetual state of being in hot water, but she didn't. She looked puzzled, but obediently drank the tea, and said nothing more until the canteen woman took the cup away, and Dr. Mann held out an arm for her to stand up.

"Better now," she said. "I can walk, I think. Where's that case?"

"Here it is," he said, picking it up. "It was all I had to identify you by, as it happens. By the way, I'm Felicity's brother Maurice—my sister has probably briefed you about me."

She nodded, and said no more till they were in the car. The porter asked her as she passed him if she were better, and the canteen woman called out to her and waved, but she just seemed dazed.

In the car, however, she said, "Who did you say you were?"

"Maurice. Felicity's brother," he said, driving carefully out of the station yard and into the main street of Latchmarket.

She stared around her. She was still very white, a curious waxy white, and now he came to think of it, she had seemed rather pale when she had got off the train, but not having seen her before, he had taken it for granted that that was her natural look.

"Where is this?" she asked suddenly.

"Latchmarket. It used to be the main market town of the county—look, you can just see the old roof of the market and the bull-ring through that street—but now of course it's been added to. It's a big industrial town now, I fear. Ugly with its prosperity."

"Where is it—what town is it near, I mean?"

"It isn't too far from Uxley Green where the hospital is, and not too far from Mortonhill and Chiverbridge. Plenty of shopping centres and bus services, if that's what you were thinking of."

She didn't answer that, and presently he was aware that she was searching in her handbag. It seemed to be a thorough and rather unsuccessful search.

He said, "What is it? Have you lost something?"

By way of answer, she said, "What did you call me just now?"

He was surprised. "Miss Moore. I hope it didn't sound too stilted, but frankly I'm not the sort of person who can leap into using a christian name on first meeting, though I'm well aware that Felicity would expect me to call you Bridget from the first moment of setting eyes on you."

She thought about that. She seemed so troubled that it penetrated through his barrier of reserve, and after a quick glance at her, he flagged down the traffic behind him and pulled into the side. "Look here, what's bothering you? If you've lost something, for heaven's sake say so, and we'll go back for it. There's time. I just wanted to get you back to the hospital for a quick check-up—one can't be too careful. You don't look very well, come to think of it."

"I don't feel very well," she admitted in a bothered tone. "But it can't be anything much, can it?"

"Have you been unwell lately?" he asked her, frowning. "Odd, I gathered from Felicity—well, I mean, she gave me

28

the impression—that you were as fit and bursting with energy as she is."

Then the girl really staggered him. "Who," she said slowly, "is Felicity?" and added blankly, "I mean, why am I being taken to her?"

"What did you say?"

His tone brought her eyes round to meet his. She was shaking all over, he noticed. "You'll think this peculiar, but I ought to tell you, I suppose, before we go any further, because you say you're a doctor so you'll know what to do. You see, I know why I fainted. It was horrible."

"Go on," he encouraged.

"Well, I got off the train and I stood there and looked round, and the most frightening thing happened to me. I read the name on the station—Latchmarket—and I'd never heard of it before and I didn't know why I was there. I couldn't remember my name. I didn't know who I was. Everything was quite blank. I was so scared, I passed out."

She looked anxiously at him. "What

happened to me?" she whispered. "Have you ever heard anything like this before?"

His smile was extremely encouraging. "Oh, yes, often. Don't worry. Your memory will come back, but fortunately for you, we know who you are. Your name is Bridget Moore."

"Bridget Moore," she repeated doubtfully. "Is it? Is it really? There's nothing at all in this handbag. That's what I was looking for just now—some means of identification."

"Well, when you get to the hospital, and change your clothes, have a look for name tabs. All your things should be marked. Oh, I suppose you've forgotten that too—you're an old friend of my young sister Felicity, who is trying rather unsuccessfully to train to be a nurse. It would appear that you agreed to come and train with her. That's why we're now going to the hospital."

She said something like, "Perhaps it's as well," under her breath, and then added, after some thought, "But shall I be accepted, now I . . . can't remember anything?"

"I expect you'll be warded for a time, for check-ups. Amnesia is nothing to be frightened of. Sometimes it rights itself. You may just need rest. I shall have to call on my sister for the sort of life you've been living, the conditions and so on."

"What causes amnesia?" the girl asked quietly.

"Several things. A blow on the head, much more usually the mind simply refusing to accept something (something worrying or unpleasant) so it just folds up and refuses to work, to put it simply."

"Like a limb, after one has been ill in bed?"

"Something like," he said kindly, then gave his attention to getting through the bottleneck that caused so much trouble with the traffic, just outside of Uxley Green.

"That big grey building ahead, behind that bank of trees, and the high yellow wall, is our hospital," he said. "St. Mary's."

"Oh. Did I really agree to go and work there?" she asked doubtfully. "It doesn't look a very friendly place."

"Actually it is. A very nice place to work in," he told her, with a quiet confidence that brought a smile to her lips.

"I think you must be prejudiced. Still, we'll see. I can but try," she said, and he noticed she had stopped trembling.

He took her to Home Sister and explained what had happened. Home Sister said she would have the newest arrival put to bed ready for him.

Bridget said, in a slightly alarmed voice, "Oh! Will *you* be examining me?"

"Of course—this is the RMO who is in charge of the health of all the nursing staff," Home Sister broke in, looking faintly shocked. "There seems to be a lot I shall have to brief you on."

It occurred to Maurice, in that moment, that Home Sister didn't really believe the amnesia story. Of course, with Felicity's record, and this was Felicity's best friend, one could hardly blame the poor woman for suspecting that this was just another bit of mischief cooked up between them to further harry her working hours.

Maurice said quietly, "Not to worry. Felicity will be there, and I shall probably bring over another doctor with me."

The girl looked more contented at that, and went quietly with Home Sister to find Felicity.

Felicity, however, was over in the hospital. She joined Maurice on his way back. "Well, brother darling, what do you think of my best friend, Bridget?"

"Rather an improbable choice for a little monkey like you," he said slowly.

"What's improbable about her? She's the most gorgeous fun, and she's not afraid of anything," Felicity said. "What have you done with her, by the way?"

"Sent her to bed. She fainted on the station."

"She wha-at?" Felicity came to a halt with astonishment. "Listen, darling, are we talking about the same person? Bridget Moore never fainted in her life!"

"Who else would we be talking about?" he asked quietly. "I'm on my way to have

33

a look at her. You'd better come too. She appears to have lost her memory, though I fancy Home Sister didn't swallow that."

Felicity grinned broadly. "She wouldn't. Neither do I, to be honest. What a perfectly glorious rag! Trust old Bridget to think up something like that, because I've recently learned, brother darling, from the small amount of information they've managed to sink into my silly little head, that amnesia is unprovable."

"Then you got it slightly wrong, my dear. The general condition can be taken into account, to the extent, for instance, of knowing whether a perfectly healthy person is faking."

"Go on, you're only saying that to scare me. All right, I know we'll be for the biggest rocket yet, if we're caught, but don't worry, my friend Bridget will think of something."

She almost danced along. Maurice thought with compunction that it was unbelievable that a girl could be so lovely, so full of life, so utterly lovable, and yet be such a hare-brained, tiresome imp into the bargain. He always felt torn in two—wanting to be with her, yet aching to be miles away, beyond the reach of her mischief.

The psychiatrist was to follow on. Maurice and his sister went up to the sick bay, and Felicity dropped to ground level on her knees, to peep round the door and surprise her friend. She no doubt expected a whoop of delight, and Maurice was surprised to find her climbing to her feet, an uncertain expression on her face.

"What is this, brother darling?" she murmured.

"Are you turning the tables on me for once?"

He'd had enough of her nonsense. "Let's go in," he said shortly.

She went in and stood by his side. She and the girl sitting up in bed, stared at each other in silence.

"Well, what is it, Felicity?" he asked uneasily.

"Who's this?" she asked in a small voice. "It's not Bridget!"

2

IT was clear that Home Sister didn't believe it. That wasn't surprising, after the way Felicity had behaved since she had been in PTS. But after a serious talk with Felicity, they all had to accept it.

Maurice said at last, "All right, so this is not Bridget Moore. What does Bridget Moore look like—now don't say you can't describe her, Felicity. You've got to—or better still, do you have a picture of her?"

"Yes," Felicity said, in surprise.

"Then why didn't you give it to me when I went to meet the train?" he asked, and for such a quiet shy man, his voice was filled with anger. Anger the more terrible to Felicity, because his voice still remained quiet, and because she had rarely seen her brother angry with her before. He usually looked resigned, annoyed, any of the milder emotions, but he never looked quite like this.

"You never asked me. Besides, it wouldn't have helped you. It isn't in colour."

"But at least we can see whether she's dark or fair, tall or short, surely?" he retorted.

Felicity was despatched to get it. They were congregated in Home Sister's office —Home Sister, Maurice, Dr. Alan West, the psychiatrist, and Felicity. Alan West, in his early forties, had a slight smile playing around his mouth as he watched Maurice's young sister demurely pass the snapshot across to Home Sister.

Felicity was right. It didn't help at all. Her friend was standing in a crowd which had parted sufficiently to show her face and head, but they were all on the beach in swim things, and Bridget's swim-cap completely hid her hair. The sun was in her eyes and she was screwing her face up, and as she had apparently just come out of the water, she had no make-up on. As neutral and unidentifiable a face as could be imagined.

Home Sister passed it to Maurice, who

passed it to Alan West. "All right, Felicity, strain your mental powers and remember what colour her hair is, if you can," Maurice said wearily.

"Darling, it's so difficult," she said, and flushed as Home Sister's eyebrows shot up at the endearment for the RMO. "I mean, last time I saw her, she was blonde, but the time before that she was black—and she doesn't always tell me when she changes the colour."

"No use asking what her natural colour is?" he asked wearily.

"Yes. Mouse brown. That's why she dyes her hair."

Alan West ducked his head, because his mouth was very difficult to control. Felicity Mann always amused him.

"So," Maurice said, with infinite patience, "I have met and brought here a total stranger with amnesia, who somehow had your case. (Why?) Your friend Bridget, who is some unspecified colour hair (any use asking what colour her eyes are? I thought not!) and who has abandoned her belongings in your old case (for heaven's sake why?), is missing. Or would she just have missed her way to the hospital, having forgotten (or never having been briefed by you) that someone would meet her?"

Felicity brightened. "Oh, yes, Maurice, she knew she was to be met—actually I sent her that old picture of you, the one you had taken ten years ago. Of course, you look centuries younger—" Felicity broke off, abashed, before Home Sister's indignant look, and amended that. "Well, it was a fairly good picture. She should have been able to recognise you from it."

Maurice reflected uncomfortably that she probably hadn't seen him because he had hidden behind the chocolate stand, but he wasn't going to say so now.

"I suppose we'd better telephone her home and find out if she really went on that train," he said.

"Well, of course she did, dar—I mean, sir," Felicity put in. "Or else my case wouldn't have been there, would it?"

"Irrefutable reasoning," Alan West

murmured to no one in particular, and Maurice glared at him.

Home Sister got out her notes. "Matron appears to know the guardian of the girl, a Colonel Partridge," she remarked, adjusting her reading glasses. "We have his telephone number here. Perhaps we should call now, sir?"

Maurice sighed. No one told him anything. He hadn't known that Bridget Moore had that illustrious traveller for a guardian. Even he himself had heard of Colonel Partridge, and he wasn't looking forward to speaking to him. He suggested that Home Sister should handle it, but she declined.

"He won't be at home," Felicity murmured, but Home Sister was asking switchboard for the call, so it had to be put through. And it so happened, Felicity found, as she stuck out her lower lip mutinously, that Colonel Partridge was very much at home. She could hear his voice bellowing down the receiver to her brother.

Maurice kept calm and explained, briefly, lucidly, politely. It did no use.

The Colonel bellowed, for even Felicity to hear plainly at the far side of the big desk, "Not arrived? But I put her on the train myself, damn it!" And as Maurice unfolded the tale, Felicity heard the older man bellow, "That damned shabby case! Some tomfoolery going on between those two girls. I don't know what!"

Felicity widened her eyes innocently as everyone looked at her. Alan West's expression was extremely reflective, and Felicity could feel her cheeks growing hot. She didn't like him much. Any man over the age of forty shouldn't look quite so handsome, nor be so sure of himself, nor make a little nurse feel distinctly unsure of herself. He was positively the only man who had ever been able to do that, and without much effort, it appeared.

Maurice, still explaining, said at last, "I'm afraid we shall have to contact the police, sir. It's a question of the other young lady, who had the case with your ward's belongings in."

41

"Your young sister's damned case!" the Colonel roared again. "Oh, look here, don't do anything foolish like calling in the police. There's always such a furore and it doesn't help. Well, to be frank, my wife has been ill—still is—don't want her upset."

Felicity breathed again. That was all right, then. Mrs. Partridge was always ill, not hospital-ill but protective-ill. That was, she retired to her room demanding quiet with curtains drawn, invalid food and maids only coming near her, to give her a rest from the Colonel.

Maurice said he didn't know how he could avoid going to the police. The answer was roared down the telephone: "Enquiry agent, of course! Much more discreet. More effective too, sometimes. Know a chap myself—get in touch, if she doesn't turn up tonight. Don't worry, nothing will happen to her. I pity the chap who'd be foolhardy enough to touch my ward Bridget. You don't know her!"

Maurice felt thankful he didn't know her. He was about to terminate the conversation when Alan West wrote on a pad and slid it in front of him. Maurice nodded, and said, "Oh, I wonder if you could tell me, sir, what your ward was wearing—the colours and all that. We shall have to enquire at the station. She might be wandering about trying to find the hospital."

The Colonel said quite clearly and distinctly, "An outfit I heartily disapprove of. Too loud! Told her so. Cream suit (madness for travelling, picks up every spot!) and ghastly oddments in bright green, terrible colour. Accessories, I believe they're called. Green shoes—frightful."

"What colour hair-dye?" the resourceful Alan West wrote on his pad and passed it across. Maurice, with considerable distaste, reframed the question: "I don't know what your ward looks like, sir —colouring and so on. Eyes, hair. Could you brief me?"

The Colonel almost exploded. "Don't talk to me about hair—dyes it. Disgraceful! Ginger, at the moment. Well, red. Eyes? Damned if I know—sometimes green, sometimes grey. Saucy baggage altogether. Get her married off, that's what I must do. Pass the buck to some other chap. Too old now. Want peace at my time of life."

Peace, Maurice considered, hardly seemed the one essential ingredient the Colonel was craving, but he murmured suitable things, raised his eyebrows at Alan West and received a shake of the head in reply, and finally rang off.

"Well, Sister," Maurice said, "where does that get us? The Colonel wants no police enquiries, but will engage an enquiry agent if this girl doesn't turn up. She has red hair, is termed a saucy baggage by her guardian, and wears very loud clothes. Surely someone must have seen her getting off that train."

"Didn't you, Maurice?" Felicity asked innocently.

"No," he said, precisely. "I wasn't looking for any young woman, I was looking for your case."

Felicity retired abashed before Alan

West's open broad smile, and was relieved to find she was dismissed. Home Sister had had more than enough of her for one day.

Alan West followed her out. "Nurse Mann!"

She skidded to a halt. "Yes, sir?"

"Quite off the record, you know where your friend is, don't you?" he said, with a swiftness and a ruthlessness that took her breath away.

"No, sir! Indeed I do not!" she said indignantly.

He looked into her eyes and after a silence he said, "Yes, I believe you're telling the truth. Well, let's put it this way —you know her well, and we don't. You must be guessing what's happened to her. For her own sake, what about letting me hear where you think she is?"

She looked hard at him. "If I do, sir, you'll tell, and we'll both get into awful trouble and it won't be nice for my brother."

"It depends on what your answer is,

doesn't it? If what she's up to is so bad, then she'll inevitably be in hot water."

Felicity looked bothered. "You don't really want me to help her get into trouble, do you, sir?"

"I like your loyalty, but think of it from our point of view—mine, your brother's, Home Sister's, ultimately Matron's and that of the hospital. If anything frightful has happened to her—"

"Oh, I don't think it has," Felicity put in swiftly.

"Then I can only conclude that you know where she is. I suggest you tell and quickly, otherwise sooner or later a lot of people are going to start an official hunt and the press and radio, to say nothing of television, will be—"

"Oh, no!" Felicity gasped. "Oh, no, that would be too awful!"

"Walk you down to the tennis courts," he said abruptly. "I'm going that way and I would like to get this cleared up. You see, we have the odd position of a quite exceptional young person, who just couldn't have been lost in a crowd—

everyone would have noticed her, a colourfully dressed redhead. People always do stare, especially if she's pretty."

"I think she is," Felicity said loyally and glumly.

"Well, then. What happened to her?"

In the hospital grounds was a small shrubbery with a little bridge over a stream. This had been part of the grounds of a private house that had been taken over and was now the Nurses' Home. Alan West stopped Felicity on the bridge. She couldn't get away from him without answering his question. She said very uncomfortably, "I daresay she got out before the train started, on her own station. I don't know, sir, but that's what I'd do."

"I see. And why would you get out before the train started, and leave a case with your belongings behind?"

Felicity shrugged. "Depends on what happened to make her change her plans."

"Well, go on, I've a lot of time at the moment. I can bear to be trifled with up to a point, when I want to know something badly enough. Let's put it this way—has she ever done this sort of thing before?"

Felicity nodded miserably. "Once."

"Tell me about it."

She glowered up at him, but he had the forceful sort of personality that suggested to her that it might be less painful in the long run to do as he desired now. She said, very unwillingly, "She put on a lot of loud colours, like now, so that people would notice her, then she went into the thing-ummy on the train and took them off and put some drab things on, no one noticed her and she got off. Just like that."

He was trying not to smile. "For what, or shouldn't I ask for fear of the terrible things I might hear?"

He was rewarded by a very suspicious look indeed, but she answered, forcing herself to be civil, because this was no second-year medical student to be trifled with, like Toby Fairbairn for instance. "She wanted to meet someone her guardian didn't want her to meet."

"I see. We seem to be getting somewhere. So you think she's gone off with an undesirable companion, and will turn up later with some cock and bull story of what happened to her."

Felicity didn't answer. There didn't seem to be any need to. He had all the answers.

He said briskly, "Well, come along, you must have some idea who she went to see. I venture to think you know all her friends and she knows yours. Close buddies, what?"

It wasn't in her to deny this, so she nodded miserably. "It could be a photographer she knows, called Eileen Shelley."

"Don't fool about with me, Nurse Mann," he said, very quietly. "I think we've both tacitly agreed that your absent friend wouldn't waste all her time, effort and ingenuity on meeting a girl friend. Try again."

"I only know a man called Frank Ulster. He's an art dealer."

"Now we're getting somewhere. Sure you don't know anyone else? Well, let's put it another way. Sure you don't know anyone else she knows, who could be prevailed on to tax their poor brains to remember who she might have met today?"

Felicity was stung then. "The essence of the whole thing, sir, was to keep it a secret—from her guardian. Well, he won't let her do anything worth doing."

"If by worth doing, you mean meeting undesirable men, I can't say I blame the poor chap, irascible as he sounded. Come on, let's get moving."

"Where to, sir?"

"To get on suitable outdoor clothes and come investigating with me, while you think of who else might know of the naughty doings of the absent Miss Moore."

"You mean—go with you, sir?"

"I do, and it will be no joy-ride, I do assure you!"

She trotted disconsolately by him. He had a very long stride, and now he was impatient. She ventured, "I can't go anywhere, sir. I'm not allowed out this week because of—well—things I did.

That was the whole point of my brother going to meet Bridget."

Alan West stopped short. "Oh, yes, that's another point we haven't cleared up. Why worry your poor brother to do something when you knew that girl wouldn't turn up?"

"But I didn't know that, sir. I'm only guessing now, because Maurice didn't find her and because something similar happened once before."

"All right. Well, scoot back to the Home and I'll have a word with Sister about getting you off the hook for just this once. And I'll have a word with your brother, so you don't use that to get out of going with me."

Maurice had gone up to the sick bay to see the girl he had brought from the station. She had a tranquillity that appealed to him very much, and even though she was now worried sick and far from well, she kept her voice controlled, pleasant, and she was very calm.

"I want you to think very carefully. Do you remember seeing anyone to answer this description, after you had got off the train?" and he told her what Bridget might reasonably look like.

She thought, and then shook her head. "It's as if I went to sleep years ago and came awake on that platform. I just can't remember a thing—don't think I haven't tried. I, too, would like to know who I am and what I was doing on that train."

"What was there in that handbag? Surely something in there would ring a bell?"

For answer, she found the bag and gave it to him. "I don't believe it's mine," she said. "Well, who would wear a black bag with a brown outfit? Besides, the make-up is for a very fair person. Everyone knows that. (Well, women would, anyway). And no lipstick, so it might reasonably belong to an older person. But although there's a small change purse, there's no note-case, and usually there's a note-case, or at least a zip pocket to put things like return tickets or appointment cards or a book of stamps, receipts and things. There's nothing. Even the hankie hasn't got a name tab."

He closed the bag. It was the most tidy, uncomplicated bag, and no personality about it. "New, too," he commented, thinking.

"A rather cheap quality bag," she added. "And no perfume. No keys, either —I've just remembered that."

"Rather as if our joking friend took your bag and supplemented a specially bought bag? Oh, no, that's too far-fetched. Well, you mustn't worry. They'll be sedating you. Perhaps after a couple of days' relaxation you'll find little things will come back. Try not to strain to remember."

"I suppose I couldn't see an evening paper?" she asked wistfully.

"No, I really don't think that would be wise," he said.

He got up to go, just as Alan West knocked and peered in. "Oh, there you are, Mann. Have I your permission to borrow your young sister, if Home Sister will release her?"

"With the greatest of pleasure, but do

you know the risks you run?" Maurice asked, with elevated eyebrows and a smile hovering round his mouth.

"The risks, dear boy, will be on the other foot. I want to make use of her, to contact the friends of the missing Miss Moore. I have a theory, boosted by your sister's apparent guilty conscience. I suppose you wouldn't care to join us for a hair-raising half hour."

"No, thanks, not even to protect you. Besides, I'm on call," Maurice said unfeelingly.

The patient listened to them going down the corridor. Her heart began to beat quickly again. She fumbled under her pillow and brought out the things she had been hiding. It was true that there had been nothing in the handbag, but when she had been left to undress, she had found some very odd things in the pockets in her clothes. There had been several pockets; in the two in the jacket were sheets of paper. One was the middle sheet of a letter, unsatisfying because there was no name of addressee or name of sender, and the second sheet was a list of rather fancy names. Horses? She frowned at it. No, rather too consistently Oriental for that.

The third thing was the oddest of all. Small—not more than four inches one way and three the other—a curious thing of great ugliness and age, and indeterminate material. It could be bone with the marks of woven thread carved into it or it could be cloth impregnated on wood. It had a strange musky smell and it filled her with repugnance. On one side was a carved design. Carved? Or burnt into the substance? Its obvious age, or semblance of age, worried her. She didn't like it and wanted to throw it away, but she dared not. It might just have the key to her identity.

She kept it grasped in one hand, while she read the other sheet, the fragment of the letter. It was written in a very bold handwriting which she felt could hardly be hers. The writer must have been a forceful personality, to judge by the wording:

". . . I just couldn't wait a moment

longer. I have to have it. I must see you. I happen to know you'll be free on Thursday. It's difficult to get away, but I'll manage somehow. R promised, but wants to back out and ES is pretty feeble when it comes to the point, but I must have . . ."

She lay back and asked herself if she could ever write so demandingly, but she didn't know herself at all. She wished she had a pencil to try out her handwriting. How could you tell what it would be like till you'd tried? But there was nothing handy and footsteps were coming. She put the pieces of paper in the handbag, but didn't have time to recover the odd thing she had been holding. It was on the edge of the sheets and as she moved it slipped down the bed.

Dr. Mann came in with a nurse. They had a kidney bowl and syringe. Dr. Mann said, "Now this will really help you. It will be nice to sink into a deep sleep. Let yourself go. Don't fight it." He held the syringe up to test it till a bead of liquid shot out and then he turned to the arm the nurse had bared ready.

With the hand of her other arm, the patient softly groped about under the bedclothes till she found the object she sought. Its cold, rather rough surface lay in her hand and she wondered how she could manage to get it put into the handbag. Would there be time after Dr. Mann and the nurse left her? She doubted it. Drowsiness was already seeping over her like a heavy, cloying blanket and her eyelids felt as if they were weighted with lead. For heaven's sake, what had been in that injection?

Her arm, lying outside the bedclothes, dropped down, and the hand gradually opened. The little dark object dropped on to the bedclothes, and later, slid down to the floor. That was after all the light had been drained from the day. Home Sister had decided to leave her patient in quiet and peace. She wouldn't want a light on. Felicity wanted to go and see the girl, but Home Sister wouldn't let her. Besides,

Alan West had already bespoken Felicity's presence.

Home Sister had been a little dubious about letting the girl go out. But Dr. Mann had given his permission and it seemed to be of some importance. Alan West had said, rather oddly, "It's no social thing, Sister, I assure you. I happen to want that young woman's help in tracing her friend. I have an idea and she might as well do the donkey work. It's time she did something useful."

With that, Home Sister heartily concurred. She also thought wistfully of a few hours without the worry of that girl around. She would be Mr. West's responsibility and he was welcome to her.

Alan West took Felicity to his cousin's office in Wilkington. The staff had gone home, but there was the advantage of a telephone with an extension. His cousin was a business woman who normally terrified him, but she agreed to stay on for the sake of propriety and because she was interested. She had a few ideas on the subject, too.

Alan said to Felicity, "Now, the art dealer. Let's get him first. Have you got his number?"

Felicity would have played him up if she'd been alone with him, but the cool, rather amused eyes of the cousin, behind impressive horn-rimmed spectacles, rather quelled her, so she gave in gracefully and consulted her little book. The art dealer was having a party.

Alan said, "There should be someone in that bunch who knows the answer, surely," and Felicity tried.

"Frank, about Bridget—" she began.

The art dealer was curiously fussed. "Now, sweetie, I had nothing whatever to do with it," he said at once.

"What are you talking about?" she asked blankly. "I only want to know who she went to meet on the train today." .

"Oh, that!" His relief was ludicrous. "She did say a new man, sweetie, but she was very cagey indeed. Wouldn't say the name or anything. Doesn't trust a soul when it comes to having secrets from her guardian, our Bridget doesn't."

"Tell him she's missing!" Alan wrote on his pad, so she did, and they got a squeak of alarm from the other end. The lightweight voice of Frank Ulster registered absolute dismay.

"Now listen, sweetie, I want nothing to do with this. When people are missing the police get called in and then where should we all be?"

"Frank darling, the police are not going to be called in. Bridget's supposed to be starting to be a nurse—"

Frank laughed. "That's as good a cover as any I know," he said.

"—and the hospital people are getting edgy because her uncle put her on that train, he says—"

"He never did! Then, sweetie, something's gone wrong since I spoke to her, because that wasn't the line at all."

"Frank, I'm worried. Please ask your friends if they know anything. It's for Bridget—her safety—"

"Well, all right. I'll call you back," he said, but when he learned that it was a trunk call, he told her to hold on instead.

He went and was back in five minutes. "Not a thing, sweetie. All my friends thought she was to meet this darling man she'd been introduced to, but that's off, but absolutely, if her guardian put her on that train. A quite, quite unreasonable man, that."

After Felicity had rung off, Alan West's cousin said, "Might one ask what sort of set-up that is?"

"What *do* you mean?" Felicity asked indignantly. "He's just an art dealer who likes a lot of parties. He can't help it if he isn't a doctor or a high-pressure business—"

"Thank you, my dear, that lowers my morale quite a lot," the cousin said, with a rueful smile. "Who do we call next?"

They called Eileen Shelley who had the photographic studio. She was furious.

"Really, Felicity, do you have to call me at this particular time? I'm trying to get a shot of a little dear aged five—"

"But it's late," Felicity said. "Don't toddlers go to sleep at this hour any more?"

"Naturally. That's why it's late. He's so sleepy that he has no fight left. At least, he hadn't till the phone rang. Now he's bawling the roof down and trying to kick my camera about the room. Hold on a minute—"

"Eileen, I only want to ask where Bridget is," Felicity said desperately.

Dead silence descended at the end of the line. "Eileen?" Felicity called.

"No can do," Eileen's thick voice said shortly, and she hung up.

"Well," Alan's cousin commented, "does she know or is she just rather cross with you for messing up a difficult assignment?"

"I don't know," Felicity said, and looked fussed. She noticed that the cousin was looking up at Alan West, who was already, in Felicity's view, looking thoroughly unfamiliar without his white coat and wearing a disreputable thick jersey with a polo collar, his hands in his trouser pockets. And he was looking at Felicity with an expression she found it hard to name.

He hates me. Well, I hate him, she told herself angrily.

"Not to worry, darlings," she said recklessly. "I have two other telephone calls yet—long distance—and I don't know who's paying for them, but—"

"Not to worry," Alan said quietly. "Not hard up."

Felicity called Rachel Argyll. While she waited for the call to be put through, Alan drawled, "I suppose it's asking too much to know where this one figures?"

"Rachel Argyll is very respectable," Felicity said with an odd dignity. "She's older than us. The big sister of Gwyneth Argyll, who knew Bridget at school. Rachel's terribly clever."

"Female QC, perhaps?" the cousin asked with gentle malice, probably knowing full well it would be nothing like that.

Felicity flushed. "She's a demonstrator of make-up, and that's a thing not everyone can be good at."

Alan frowned at his cousin. Felicity was

loyal, at least. She didn't like her friends decried.

Rachel Argyll had a sleepy, syrupy voice that Alan and his cousin hated. "Listen, darling, of course I know where Bridget is, but neither she nor Neil will want it shouted around. You know what the guardian is like, and they're only doing a show somewhere. She'll turn up all right, don't worry."

"Well, if that's all, why didn't she let me know?" Felicity fumed. "I'm her best friend, aren't I? I was worried. I thought she was engaged in something ghastly, the way everyone was going on."

"Everyone?" Rachel was guarded now.

"Well, Frank and Eileen."

"Oh. Listen, honey, Bridget has her own life to live. You can't live it for her. Just leave her alone, if you want my advice."

"But suppose something has happened to her?" Felicity persisted.

"Nothing will happen to Bridget," Rachel said, and rang off.

"How can she be so sure?" said Felicity, half to herself.

Alan West raised his eyebrows at his cousin. She leaned back, a stocky woman in her late forties, with shrewd eyes and a keen mind. She looked at Alan and at Felicity's dewy freshness, and half smiled, but it was of Rachel Argyll that she spoke. "There's a female with a load to hide."

"How can you say that?" Felicity burst out.

"You like her?"

"I like all my friends and all Bridget's friends," Felicity said hotly, and privately added that she didn't care much for Alan West's cousin. He had the cousin he deserved.

Alan said, "Well, it's all we can do, I suppose. Oh, just a minute—this Neil she mentioned. Who would that be?"

Felicity didn't know and said so, bluntly. By now she was rather hurt with Bridget for keeping so much from her. Bridget wrote once a week, all about her doings, her battles with her guardian, her compassion for his wife, and her own secret thoughts. But nothing had been said at all in those letters to lead Felicity to expect any of this.

Alan nodded at her denial. Unlike his cousin, he believed Felicity was telling the truth and he could sense her hurt. She wouldn't want to be questioned any more now. He thanked his cousin for her help and loan of the office and he took Felicity away.

"Shall we partake of some refreshment?" he asked her with an odd dignity. "A coffee would do me, but I'm not very au fait with what the PTS drink nowadays."

She would have sadly liked a fierce concoction called South Sea Island Dream, which the PTS had made up in Barney's Milk Bar round the corner, but the mere mention of ice-cream or cold drinking chocolate would bring that supercilious smile to the corners of his mouth. Besides, she told herself, he was old. Too old to remember what it was like to enjoy a sweet drink.

She said, with a fine carelessness, "We

66

also drink coffee," but added hastily that as she was in disgrace, she had better go right back, so that she could look Home Sister straight in the eye and say she had done nothing else but attend to the business required of her.

"Do you always look people in the eye when you tell the truth?" Alan asked, with unusual gentleness.

"Yes. If I can't look them in the eye, I say 'I'm sure I couldn't say'."

"I see, Nurse Mann. Then I'll remember that." And he took her back to the Nurses' Home without further argument.

She shared a room with Ann Taylor, who was brainy and plain and wore glasses: Kathy Milburn who was quiet, not brainy but ambitious and who worked like two people to achieve the required result —and Linda Howland, who was sport-minded and muddled through her lessons. They were all working too hard to want to talk, and they turned in early.

Felicity lay in her bed near the window

and thought about the things that had happened to her today.

Yesterday she frolicked through and landed flat on her face in another scrape and was given yet another chance, but life had still been pure uncomplicated fun.

Today everything had changed. Bridget, who should have joined her, was missing. A stranger, who had the oddest effect on her brother, to judge by the way he looked at her, had come in Bridget's place, and the wretched girl was supposed to have amnesia. Somehow it concerned Bridget, and the worst of it all was that Bridget had not been confiding in her. That broke a long friendship, surely, when one party got into bad trouble and hadn't confided in the other? Worse, Bridget had pretended to be giving confidences in all those letters of hers.

Those letters . . . It was suddenly imperative to read them all again, just to see if anything in them that she had previously missed should come to light now. She could find them with her torch, read them under the bedclothes with her torch. Perhaps reading Bridget's letters would help at least to chase away the nasty shaken feeling she got when Mr. West looked at her the way he did, Felicity told herself.

She found the letters, but she stopped to look out of the window through the gap in the curtains. It was so nice out there—tempting enough to go out on to the flat roof, so she wouldn't have to be careful about waking the others. But she just hadn't the nerve. The flat roof was out of bounds, anyway.

As she was moving away from the window, a movement down in the patch of moonlight caught her eye. It was a girl!

Felicity couldn't believe it. It must be one of the PTS shut out and trying to attract attention. Whoever it was had moved back into the shadows, but this seemed to the restless Felicity as good an excuse as any to rustle up the nerve to go out on to the flat roof.

It was two floors down, and out of the fire door. She put on a jersey and slacks over her pyjamas and quietly let herself out of the bedroom and sped downstairs in bare feet. The corridors of the Home were still and shadow-filled, the uncurtained windows letting in enough light from the moon to see by.

The fire door squeaked a little, but nothing happened, so she crept out, and lay flat on her tummy overlooking the edge.

There was the movement again, plainer now, down at this lower level. A girl moved out of the shadows in response to Felicity's raised arm.

She fled across the moonlit patch, that girl in mufti down there, and stood in shadow for a second before climbing the ladder that was fixed to the wall. As her face came up level with Felicity's, a voice Felicity knew well said, "Who says miracles don't happen? I wished and wished you'd appear, and you looked out of the window!"

"*Bridget!*" Felicity gasped.

3

"**B**RIDGET! What on earth are you doing here?" Felicity gasped. "Why didn't you come with my brother? He did come to meet you off that train."

"I know it," Bridget said. "Don't be silly. I saw him, hiding behind the chocolate machine. If you want to know, I can't stand men who do that. Shy men give me the willies."

"You *are* a clot! He brought someone else back with him and she doesn't know who she is. *Now* what are we going to do?"

"Listen, that's what I wanted to talk to you about," Bridget said urgently. "I'm in terrible trouble."

"What, again?" Felicity said weakly. Trouble was Bridget's middle name, but Felicity had rather hoped it wouldn't be so bad that they couldn't laugh over it together. She also knew Bridget well enough to know that this was really bad trouble. "Since your last letter to me?" she was stung to ask. She still couldn't get over Bridget not confiding in her.

"Of course, or I'd have told you in my letters, silly," Bridget said at once. Felicity almost fell off the flat roof in sheer dizzy relief. It was all right between them, just as it had always been! In such a mood she was prepared to do anything for her friend, promise anything, jeopardise her future even.

"I'm coming down," she said. "We've got to talk. I suppose you know you've got the whole hospital by the ears?"

"Oh, help, why?" Bridget could never see that her doings could upset other people. She fervently believed that every person was a single entity, a law unto herself.

She helped Felicity down the last three rungs and commented, "You've got bare feet."

"Not to worry, darling—the grass isn't wet. Ugh, isn't it horrid, though? I think

I trod on a worm. Let's go over to the tool shed where no one will hear us talk. It isn't locked."

They found a dry sack in there and sat down cross-legged. Bridget had some chocolate which they munched while they talked.

"It all started last night," she began. "I had a thumping row with my guardian."

"Oh, that old thing! I wondered, darling," Felicity said. Suddenly it was all right. Clarified, it simply meant that Bridget was scoring off the Colonel. Felicity could understand that. At eighteen, she still hadn't grasped the essential law of civilised living, that there must be the two sides; authority and obedience, seniors and juniors, those with the ability to rule, those with no ability to rule. Right and wrong was still as elastic a combination to her as it had been in the junior school. Life was not a thing one owed a duty and loyalty to; it was a thing to be enjoyed to the full.

"Yes, well, it got uncomfortable. He quite unfairly said I would be upsetting

Aunt Dolly, which isn't true. She had taken the new bottle of Madeira to bed with her to comfort her, and I'm quite sure that even if our voices penetrated right up to her room (which I doubt) she would probably be too happy and sleepy to notice. I think she's got the best idea, you know; the quick and easy way to get away from it all. Me, I take the hard way and look where it's got me! I took the perishing thing and now I've lost it."

Felicity worked through all that at lightning speed, through long experience in sifting the essential from Bridget's speeches, and deftly ignoring the subject of the elderly Dorothy Partridge, she alighted on the topic most important to herself. "What perishing thing?" she asked carefully.

"Well, it's just a . . . a thing," Bridget said vaguely. "About so big," and she sketched with her hands an object that might have been anything between three inches square and a foot square. "I don't know what you call it or what it's for. I only know my guardian sets a frightfully big store by it, so I took it—just to teach him to leave me alone. I was going to put it back," she said hastily.

"Why didn't you, darling?" Felicity asked practically. It was not among her vices to touch what didn't belong to her, not from any particular scruples, but because it never interested her to do so. There would ensue tiresome trouble which wasn't worth it, so she dismissed such things from her complicated existence and concentrated on doing what would bring some sort of enjoyment by way of reward.

"I forgot, because this other thing boiled up."

"What other thing?"

"Actually left-over trouble from something else I did three weeks ago. Well, I thought the flipping letter was addressed to me. It looked like it, first go. Actually it said 're: Miss Bridget Moore' and the 're' bit had got smudged. Anyway, it was *about* me from some solicitor, and before I got far enough to find out just what it was about, my guardian came into the room, so I bunked, dropping the letter. Well, the clot has taken all this time to find out who opened it and took a peep and he was letting me have it hot and strong, and he wouldn't listen to me or else I could have told him that it isn't possible, if you open a letter by a mistake and find it's about yourself, to resist the temptation to read on. Well, would *you* have resisted?"

"No, darling," Felicity said at once, without thinking. Loyalty demanded the denial, but on second thoughts Felicity was inclined to the view that she might, for safety's sake, have made quite sure who the letter was addressed to, from the first, before being daft enough to tear it open.

"Well, where was I? Oh, yes, he decided to tell me what was in it (well, what he *said* was in it) and it wasn't very nice. It seems a lot of money was stashed away for me in share things and they've slumped horribly, so I'm hard up and on his bounty, as he put it. Hence the absolute need for this hospital thing, which I wouldn't have entertained at all if you hadn't invited me and promised it would be a lark. Actually the guardian said no larks or else something really nasty by way of fate would befall me."

"Is he hard up?" Felicity asked promptly.

"No, he can't be. I know for a fact that some of those very peculiar things he brought back from the East fetch fabulous sums at the hands of unsuspecting rich bods who like to buy things no one else has got. Funny thing, that. Why would anyone want to buy that peculiar thing I took (well, borrowed and meant to put back) and don't say I haven't got it right because he said to Aunt Dolly only the day before, that this American—"

"Which American?"

"Oh, I don't know. Van der Something or other, his name was. Well, he wanted the thing and was offering thousands of dollars—but thousands—for it, just to take the thing back to the States and swank to his friends that he'd got something they hadn't. And now it's gone."

"Where did you have it last?" That was always the question Felicity's old nurse asked her when she complained of having lost something.

"On the train," Bridget said glumly. "Well, don't look at me like that! It was in my skirt pocket. I always get interrupted when I'm doing something, and our housekeeper came into the room when I was opening the glass case it was in. So I ducked behind a cabinet, shoved the thing in my pocket and waited till she went out. She'd only come in to draw the curtains against the sun, so the mangy old treasures shouldn't fade. Who'd care, anyway?"

"A bloke from the States, darling, with more cash than sense," Felicity pointed out. "Well, what happened on the train?"

"Oh, yes, I must tell you about that. There was this gorgeous handsome he-man—"

"Which one, darling?" Felicity prompted patiently.

"Absolutely heavenly, you'd have adored him. Tall and dark and somehow a little sinister. We got talking—"

"Just a minute, I thought you were

supposed to be doing a show with Neil Baxter?"

"How did you know that?" Bridget asked, disappointed.

"I told you, darling—everyone's gone mad, looking for you, only your guardian said specially not to call in the police, so people are asking routine questions themselves. Well, the doctors and Matron and people like that, and they made me ring up anyone who might know you, so I called up one or two people, and Rachel Argyll said you didn't want the guardian to know about Neil and that you'd turn up, but, darling, I didn't think you'd turn up so late. How come Neil didn't deliver you earlier?"

"Like I'm trying to say, Neil couldn't come, so I got on the train (well, the guardian put me on, but I was supposed to look out for Neil boarding it further down, only he sent someone with a message to say it was all off after the guardian had gone), and there was this other man and he made up for Neil not being there, and—well, to be honest, I put my hand in my pocket for my hanky and the Thing fell out and this Claude Langley (that was his name) went absolutely mad over it and wanted to keep it."

"What was he, an antique dealer in disguise?"

"Don't be silly, he said his father had been out East and collected these things, and he was in hot water with the old man and he wanted to put it right somehow and would I take a fiver for it so he could give it to his father and square him."

"It's because you look so daft that people put such propositions to you," Felicity said kindly. "Not to worry. I take it you told him you'd pinched it and the coppers would be after you any minute?"

"Well, no, but I did say it wasn't mine and I'd meant to put it back before my guardian found out," Bridget said happily.

Felicity dashed her happiness. "Which promptly told him what he wanted to know, that it was valuable and worth his while to nick it from you. You get brighter, darling, the older you get."

"I told you I was in trouble," Bridget

said sadly. "You see, he got a bit insistent. We were in the corridor and someone pushed by, and he put his arm round me and tried to pinch it from my pocket, only he wasn't slick enough. He even tried to kiss me while he tried to get it. I wasn't having that."

"Clever old you! So you hid it? Where, in the thingummy, I bet, and then you forgot which one."

"No, not quite. I pushed it down the back of my seat in the compartment before he took me to the restaurant car. I left your old case there to mark the spot, but when I came back your case was gone, so I couldn't be sure which compartment it was in. I tried as many as I could, but I couldn't comb the whole train."

"Lumme!" Now Felicity was sitting up looking awed. "I haven't told you yet. My clot of a big brother was supposed to nab the girl carrying the case (which he did) only it wasn't you but this other one, and she passed out, and by the time he'd got her back to the hospital she'd come to and said she couldn't remember who she was.

I thought it was a glorious bit of fun on your part, but when they made me go to the bod in sick bay, I nearly fell through the floor when I saw it wasn't you."

"Oh, lord," Bridget said in an awed voice. "Now what are we going to do?"

Felicity sat thinking. "You didn't say what happened to you since that train came in at four today."

"Oh, that! Well, I went out into the town and found a big store and they had a ladies' room, so I tidied up."

"I see you got rid of the cream and green outfit," Felicity remarked.

Bridget chuckled. "Did that trick once before, didn't I? And you remembered."

"What happened to it?"

Bridget said, in a surprised voice, "Put it in your case, of course."

Felicity sighed. "Aren't we daft? Why didn't one of us think to search that case? I bet it's just been put in the cupboard, like all the belongings of unknown patients. What happened after that?"

"I got some tea in the restaurant and had a think."

Felicity, with tremendous restraint, forbore to ask 'what with' and waited.

"As I see it," Bridget went on, furrowing her brow in an attempt at coherent thought, "someone ought to telephone my guardian to say they've seen me around so they know I'm all right."

"He doesn't seem to care. He said no harm would come to you."

"I know that, silly, but I want Aunt Dolly to know I'm all right, otherwise she'll worry."

"Poor thing," Felicity commiserated. "And then?"

"Someone'll have to find me a place to hide and bring me food and smuggle me in to get the occasional bath."

"Oh, no," Felicity said at once. "No can do, darling. I'm in hot water, figuratively, of course, at the moment, and there's a quite horrid psychiatrist friend of my big brother who keeps giving me a very peculiar look. He's gunning for me. I'm not going to give him the chance on a plate. No, as I see it, we shall have to be much more logical. What's wrong with you coming to the front door of the Nurses' Home and saying you were taken ill—"

"Who, me?"

"Yes, darling, I see what you mean. A more disgustingly healthy specimen never breathed. Well, I've got it—your story will be that you saw an old friend of your aunt and she invited you to her house and you stayed the night and turned up at the hospital next day because you didn't want to stay any longer away from starting your training as a nurse."

"Who, me?" Bridget said again.

"Don't keep saying that," Felicity fretted. "Oh, help, there must be some story we can cook up."

"How about telling the truth?" a strange voice said, and a tall shadow blocked the now open door of the shed.

After the first shocked silence, the two girls scrambled to their feet, as the newcomer flicked on a powerful torch. In the glow they could see standing behind the torch the tall figure of Alan West.

"How did you know we were here, sir?" Felicity gasped.

"You have bare feet," he said. "Do you want to get a chill?"

"Oh, I shan't," Felicity said impatiently. "How—?"

"I heard voices," he said briefly. He didn't think it necessary to explain that he had been walking over from the hospital where he had been talking to Maurice Mann, who was still on duty, and that Felicity had been so much in his thoughts that Alan had been tempted to stand still, enjoying the night air and the quiet, and staring up at the top windows of the Home where the PTS babes were (or should have been) fast asleep, and wondering if Felicity's face in slumber still held that endearing innocent look. If these girls ever found out that he was so vulnerable, he told himself, they would make mincemeat of him.

"I daresay if I hadn't come here," he went on, "half the hospital would have heard those voices, the row you were both

85

making. Well, is this the missing Bridget Moore?"

They looked at each other and turned to him. Felicity said, "Yes, it is, but she's in trouble and I really think she ought to lie low for a bit, sir!"

"Do you? I've got news for you. I never did believe in concealment, prevarication, lying your way out of trouble or any of the other things you've been turning over in those horrid little minds of yours. Now come on, both of you—shut up this shed, and back to Home Sister you're both going, and I shall personally accompany you both, to see you don't forget to do just that."

There was a silence and he wondered uneasily what he would do if they point blank refused to budge. He wouldn't have admitted it for worlds, but eighteen-year-old girls terrified him. His only hope was handling them one at a time. It took quite a bit of nerve to lecture them when he was forced to.

Felicity said, with another of those slanting looks at her friend, "All right, we'll go. I don't mind turning up with you and my best friend, but Home Sister will be livid at being turned out in hair curlers and her old dressing-gown. Actually," she said, running the tip of a pink tongue round that lovely mobile mouth of hers, "I was going to knock her up and tell her some of the truth, the bit about seeing someone in the grounds and coming down as far as the flat roof to see who it was. And then I thought maybe Bridget here (who was going to do this anyway only she wanted to tell me about it first) would go and knock on the front door and say she'd been delayed getting here, which I expect was true, only she hadn't got round to telling me what kept her."

He didn't know whether he wanted to shake Felicity or to hug her. Her duplicity and guile were terrifying, yet she looked so sweet standing there trying to talk herself and her friend out of trouble while at the same time apparently struggling to stick to the truth. He succumbed to her charm sufficiently to ask, "I don't think

I've ever heard what happened to her at all, have I?"

Bridget said, "I daren't face my guardian. Even if you make me go to the Nurses' Home I shall run away, you know, before they can fetch him. I'm in dead trouble."

Felicity tried to kick her without Alan West seeing. "She means he's pretty fed up with her already and she lost something on the train, and that's how she missed my brother, and there'll be another row about that, because her guardian's a colonel—"

"I know," Alan said dispassionately.

"—and he doesn't believe in keeping people waiting or losing things or making a hash of a time-table or anything like that."

There was a heavy silence, and just as Felicity was about to give up and admit that they were for the high jump and being thrown out of the hospital, to say nothing of a frightful row with Maurice, and upsetting the grandparents who were really rather sweet, reprieve came. Heavy footsteps clumped across the turf from the side path. It was the gardener.

"Sh-h!" Felicity cautioned, as Bridget gave a scared squeak. "Let's keep quiet till he goes."

But he didn't go. He muttered something to himself, which sounded like a few ill-chosen words about his own growing carelessness in leaving the shed unlocked, then the door was slammed to and the key turned. The gardener clumped away again and the silence was so thick, it almost smothered them.

Then Bridget started to giggle, rather hysterically and decidedly helplessly. "We're all locked in together, all of us," she said.

Felicity saw what she meant, and at once golden possibilities yawned in front of them. It was just a question of keeping one's head and working them out for the best.

Alan West saw what she was thinking in exactly the same moment. "Good grief, I want my head searching! How did I get in this predicament?" he fumed.

Felicity said innocently, "What predicament, sir? You were only trying to persuade us to go to the Home. It isn't your fault that the gardener locked us in, is it?"

"Oh, no, and it won't be my fault if the whole hospital is laughing at me for weeks," he snapped, and even Felicity was momentarily intimidated by the fury in his voice. "If ever a girl asked to be taken across someone's knee and walloped, it's you, young woman!"

"No!" Felicity said, in a scared voice. "If you touch me, Dr. West, I shall yell the place down. I'll tell my brother. I'll—"

"Your brother looked as if he might be contemplating the same form of punishment for you, when I saw him last," Alan snapped. "Give me a hairpin or something, one of you."

"What for?" Bridget asked him.

"To pick the lock—or do you imagine I intend to stay the night here with you two, until someone finds us in the morning?"

"It's a good thing we're only PTS babes

90

and not staff nurses," Felicity was unwise enough to say, but from the look he gave her in the light of his torch, she shrank back and said no more. And presently he got the door open.

"Now then, I'm going to do the sporting thing," he said. "I'm going to turn my head and look the other way while you get back into the Home the way you came out (and I don't want to know how that was!), and if you get caught after that, it's on your own head," he told Felicity. "As to you, young woman, you're coming with me to the callbox outside the gates, to telephone Home Sister and tell her any story you like to explain your delay, but ask her if you can come in tonight. And I shall be watching. Not until you're within the doors of the Home am I going to leave you. Get me?"

They both agreed that they did.

"I advise you both to forget about this night, for your own comfort as well as mine. Let's not have a repetition of it, either. I may not be so good-natured next time."

It wasn't good nature, Felicity privately thought, as she shinned up the wall ladder and padded across the flat roof. It was simply because they were both in each other's hands. They could easily spread the story of his having been locked in the gardener's shed with two PTS babes after dark, and having to pick the lock to get out, but if a whisper of it got around, he would feel free to tell everyone how he had found them, out of bounds, cooking up a suitable story, and Bridget up to the eyes in trouble, anyway. Felicity paused, in sudden fright, both to test the door from the flat roof in case someone had locked it, and to wonder how much he had heard of their conversation before he had joined in.

She barely had time to reach her shared room before the telephone started to ring, down in the hall.

In the silence it seemed loud enough to wake the entire Home. Home Sister wouldn't be pleased.

She was cold and tired. Whatever was the outcome now, she wouldn't see Bridget any more tonight. She fell asleep wondering where Home Sister would put Bridget to sleep.

In the morning she threw on her clothes. The others looked blankly at her. "What's the matter with you, Mann?" Ann asked nervously. She was always nervous with someone like Felicity, who apparently didn't care about anything, and who was related to the RMO anyway.

Kathy Milburn remarked, "You look terrible. Didn't you sleep very well?"

Linda was doing her early morning exercises. Her splendid young figure was well displayed as she lay flat on her back with her legs slowly arching above her head until they touched the floor behind her. "You need to do some jerks, Mann. Try it with me. It's super!"

Felicity said sourly, "No time. Got to see a man about a white monkey," and tore out of the room and down the corridor.

"She'll get thrown out before long, mark my words," Linda remarked, but the other two weren't listening. They were busy muttering the notes they had crammed into their heads the night before.

Felicity couldn't see Bridget anywhere. Risking another rocket, she shot out of the Home and across to the hospital, meaning to ask her brother if she could find him. Maurice was her last resort now. She had never been so scared in her life before, for she had now had time to recollect that Alan West had interrupted them just when Bridget had been going to tell her how she had spent the time after she had had tea, and what she had done on the train journey, besides losing the valuable object that the colonel had probably by now found to be missing.

Maurice was nowhere. Probably gone off duty. But Alan West was very much in evidence. He stopped Felicity and he looked thunderous.

"Oh, please, sir, not now. I'm looking for Bridget. I haven't seen her since— well, *you* know."

"Are you sure you haven't seen her?" he rapped out.

"No. Home Sister hasn't sent for me as

I expected her to, and I got all worked up and then . . . nothing! I don't even know where she got put to sleep last night."

"Neither do I," he said grimly. "I was hoping you could enlighten me."

Something in his manner made her heart start beating with such big powerful strokes that she could hardly breathe. What had gone wrong now?

"Me, sir?" she whispered.

"Yes, you, Felicity, and I'm not sure you can't tell me a lot more than you're pretending. Are you trying to tell me you don't know what happened after we left you?"

She shook her head, whitening.

"Well, I'll tell you. I put you both on your honour, and what happened? Someone called me, so I told her to scoot to the telephone box. I hardly wanted to be found with her in tow. And when I was free I went there. But of course, there was no sign of your precious friend. Gone, and I haven't seen or heard from her since."

4

FELICITY wasn't at all surprised to be sent for by Matron. She wondered why it hadn't happened before.

As Matrons went, this one wasn't a bad one, so Felicity had heard. From her brother she had had tales of two pretty fierce ones in his earlier hospitals, and from the big sister of one of the PTS babes she had had grim tales of a very elderly matron who had been on the point of retirement and thought she'd tidy up discipline before she handed over to the newcomer. Felicity thanked her stars there wasn't someone like that at St. Mary's.

Matron asked her to sit down and said quietly that she wanted a little talk with her.

Felicity knew all about 'little talks'. She had had a terrible life at school, in her opinion, and it had been punctuated by 'little talks' from one adult in authority after another. She sat resigned and studied Matron's face across the big desk.

Matron had rather nice light brown hair, set in a modern style beneath her much-frilled starchy cap. It was one of the few faces, Felicity considered, that didn't look soppy above the frilly bow of the cap, and moreover, Matron had a really nice figure beneath the navy silk dress. But Felicity also noted with misgivings the determined chin, the very straight look in those blue eyes, and the high clever forehead. Not for nothing had this particular Matron earned the name of No-Nonsense Norrington. She sighed. Wouldn't it be her luck to have this happen to her?

Matron said, "You are the young sister of our RMO," and she made it sound like an accusation, as if she sympathised with Maurice for being stuck with such a little horror. "But," she continued, "on this occasion I propose to forget that and to treat you as if you were any other girl working hard to get through the PTS examination and to wear the blue and green striped dress of the first-year nurses, a uniform of which we are very proud."

Felicity found for the first time that she wasn't going to like losing the comfort and protection of the lilac overall and cap of the PTS. It was a barrier. No one could really accuse one of being a nurse while one was wearing that thing.

"Now," Matron said, "I ask you to consider the nursing staff from the point of view of the relatives of a very ill patient —any sick patient. Would you not feel rather uneasy if there were things being said about curious goings-on among the young ones, when quite clearly they should be living a sober life, giving their attention primarily to learning how to tend the sick?"

Felicity's eyes widened. Matron had unerringly made her feel guilty, all kinds of a rotter. What would the grandparents say? They were such dears, and so kind to people, especially the sick and helpless of their district. Only now were they both thinking of giving up their lifelong duty of being useful to the community.

"Yes, Matron," Felicity agreed.

"Then let's see if we can straighten out this tiresome and rather boring business. How would you like to tell me, in your own words, your side of it."

"I wouldn't know where to begin, Matron," she faltered.

"The beginning is a good place. This friend of yours—Bridget Moore—when did you first meet her? At school?"

This was something Felicity could handle. She brightened. "Oh, yes, Matron, ages and ages ago—well, when we were only ten and both feeling frightfully homesick and everyone else had a best friend and no one wanted us, and we agreed that everything could be rather fun if we stuck together, and so we did. Ever since."

"I like loyalty and friendship," Matron approved. "Long friendships in particular," and then she proceeded to tear this one apart in such a way that Felicity didn't even notice until it was too late. "What is she like, this girl?"

"Oh, fun," Felicity said fervently.

"Fun," Matron repeated, considering the word. "Loyal? Kind? Honest?" Felicity nodded hard to the first and last, but wavered a little over 'kind' as a description of Bridget. In all honesty, Felicity felt that if Bridget had been kind she had kept it well hidden. Not that she was unkind, she struggled to tell herself; just too thoughtless to be anything in particular.

"I see. What are her hobbies?" Matron continued, but Bridget had none. "Sport, perhaps?" But Bridget was too stupid really to be any good at anything, except thinking up the most gorgeous jokes, practical ones, and Felicity hardly felt that Matron would want to hear that.

"I see," Matron said again. "But of course, she would be good at something," and she shuffled some papers in front of her, with a frown. Felicity, with a sinking heart, saw that they were headed reports from her old school, about Bridget presumably.

"Well, as I have no note of scholastic brilliance and you cannot tell me (and you of all people should know this) if the absent Bridget Moore has any hobbies or ability where games are concerned, one may only conclude that she has great personal charm, to claim allegiance from an intelligent girl like you."

She's getting at me, and at Bridget, Felicity told herself, and went mulish. "I like her," she muttered.

"Well, some people do like someone else without quite knowing why," Matron commiserated, and dismissed that angle. "Now we come to the record of Bridget Moore which concerns us—that is, the hospital. She was particularly given a chance to be a student nurse because you wished it so badly, and your brother, as RMO, used his position, I fear, to persuade me to accept a girl for the PTS who had no particular qualifications to justify our wasting time and money trying to train her up to ward standard."

Felicity went hot. She could see, rather belatedly, what sort of 'little talk' this was going to be.

"So far as I have been briefed, by one

person and another," Matron continued, "Bridget Moore annoyed her guardian yet another time, so that there were high words between them just before she started out for the hospital, and her guardian, after putting her on the train himself, has no further knowledge of her whereabouts. I understand she was wearing the most unsuitable clothes, and that close friends of hers in her home district believed her to be contemplating meeting a friend of the other sex, of whom her guardian would certainly not have approved."

Someone's been talking all right, Felicity thought angrily. Maurice? Or Dr. West? And of course, because she didn't like Alan West, it was inevitable that she should decide he was the culprit.

"Are we agreed so far, Nurse Mann?" Matron insisted, and Felicity nodded.

"Can you tell me something about the curious business of your brother going to the station and returning with a total stranger, thinking she was your friend?"

That surprised Felicity. Matron must

surely know that much. If she had stopped to think, she would have realised that the other information had probably been given to Matron by the Colonel himself, and not by Maurice or Alan West. But she was not in a thinking mood, just an angry, trapped kind of mood that wouldn't let her use her head.

"I wasn't able to go and meet her, Matron, so I asked my brother. That's all I know."

"I see. Well now, it seems to me that you and I have managed to get at cross purposes somewhere. I wanted to try and straighten this thing out, for the peace of mind of everyone. Home Sister, Sister Tutor, yourself and myself, your brother, Dr. West, who has tried so hard to help, and your friend, to say nothing of her guardian and his sick wife, and of course your own grandparents. Such a lot of people dependent on the rather juvenile antics of a rather selfish young woman, who has no more serious thoughts in her head than how to achieve a vanishing trick on a train by having her hair dyed and

103

using two sets of clothes," and the way Matron said it, so quietly, so disdainfully, it really did make Bridget sound as if she had been behaving pretty shabbily.

Felicity was staggered. Up till now, she had regarded Bridget as the "tops", and looked forward to her letters every week as the mainstay of her existence. She remembered with surprise, too, how hurt she had been to think that Bridget had not been quite frank with her, had not given her her complete confidence. In a few short pithy well-chosen sentences, Matron had shattered Felicity's idol.

"Let us waste no more time, Nurse Mann. What is this all about?" Matron asked, quietly dropping her carefully aimed shell.

Felicity gulped. "I . . . I honestly don't know, except that it started out like her guardian thought—a train trip with a man-friend. She honestly doesn't mean any harm—"

She stopped, asking herself now whether that was quite true. No, well, Bridget didn't mean any harm because she never bothered to think that far. She entered into things without a thought of how they would turn out.

"Yes?" Matron prompted.

Felicity was at a loss to know how to go on, without disclosing that she had already met Bridget, but there was that telephone call last night, that she had thought was Bridget telephoning Home Sister, as Dr. West had told her to.

It would have to come out, she supposed, and rather sooner than later. "She thought her friend would be on the train, only at the last minute he wasn't, so she got talking to someone else and—well, to be frank, she'd borrowed something from home and then lost it on the train, and she was scared stiff that she'd have to face her guardian before she found it. I talked with her last night—she's all right, honestly—"

Matron sat upright in her chair. "You *talked* with her?"

Felicity nodded miserably. "Only she couldn't stop. I don't know where she is or who she's staying with, but she'll be all right because the family have friends in the district and—"

"I must telephone the Colonel. The poor man is worried sick!" Matron lifted the receiver and asked for Bridget's guardian to be contacted at once, then she turned to Felicity.

"Why didn't you tell anyone about this?" she asked, and Felicity wilted under her tone.

She didn't know what to say. She had made a mistake about Alan West. It now seemed that he hadn't sneaked to Matron. Now what was she going to do? If she told her part in last night's escapade, Alan West's part in the affair would come out, and then what would happen to Felicity herself? There had been some sort of bargain that he wouldn't tell if she and Bridget didn't.

"I was afraid of getting anyone into trouble, Matron," she said at last, in a prim little voice that made Matron want to smack her.

Matron's call came through, so she dismissed Felicity and picked up the receiver. Felicity bolted while there was a chance.

On the way back to the Nurses' Home she ran into Maurice. "You're looking pretty ghastly. Are you in trouble again?"

Felicity regarded her brother sourly.

"I'm in it as deep as I can be. Just got a rocket from Matron." She thought for a moment, then she said, "Oh, I suppose you won't know. I saw Bridget last night."

He skidded to a halt and faced her. "You *whaat?*"

"Didn't Dr. West tell you? I thought he'd sneaked to Matron, so I had to tell her, but it seems he didn't. Oh, crumbs, he'll skin me if he finds out I've said, but I had to, didn't I? Anyway, she's telephoning Bridget's guardian now to tell him Bridget's all right."

"Good grief, what's going *on?*" the normally quiet Maurice exploded.

"Well, I don't know what Dr. West will say, I'm sure," Felicity said miserably, "but he caught us last night when we were outside talking, and he said he'd look the other way while I got back in the Home, if Bridget would go and knock at the front door and give herself up. Only it seems she got away and he was absolutely in a rage about it this morning when he saw me. It wasn't my fault, and I don't know where she is now."

Maurice said, in that terrible quiet voice of his that she had encountered the day before, "I think if I live to be a hundred I shall never stop being sorry I consented to go and meet that train yesterday. Don't you ever ask me to do something for you again, will you?" and he, too, marched off and left her, just as Alan West had, this morning. Felicity began to have the sneaking feeling that it would be like this in the future, if she didn't do something about Bridget's mad-hat schemes soon.

Funny, she mused, it hadn't been like this at school. One got into a row for a thing and it was forgotten, but here they were different. They took things so seriously. Well, she conceded, remembering Matron's remarks at the beginning of her interview, perhaps it was more serious here, because of all the sick people.

Felicity's troubles weren't over, either. The PTS were due to go on a trip to a farm to study hygiene in connection with milk production, and it had suddenly been arranged for that afternoon. Felicity forgot she was confined to barracks, as it were, for the rest of the week, and thought wistfully of an afternoon out. Home Sister dashed her hopes.

"You will be exempted from the trip, Nurse Mann," she ordered.

"Will I have to stay here all alone, Sister?" she asked blankly.

"No, I fear that won't be possible. You can't be trusted to behave without supervision. To that end, you will report to Sibylla Stansfield Ward in the Medical Wing, and make yourself generally useful. And I shall require a detailed account of just how useful you managed to be."

Felicity's heart sank. The old Medical Wing again! All those old women who laughed at her, and drooled over Maurice as if he were their long-lost son!

The ward Sister was away, and the staff nurse not in such a good mood today. She regarded Felicity sourly. "I've heard about your latest scrape, Mann, and I don't want any nonsense this afternoon. And keep away from that patient."

"Which patient, Staff?" Felicity asked blankly.

"That one—the girl with no memory," the staff nurse said. And Felicity looked down the ward to where the staff nurse had indicated with a jerk of the head.

"Oh, golly, the one Maurice brought back by mistake!"

"Yes," was the rather tight-lipped answer. "I heard about that, too. In the doghouse all round, aren't you?"

"That's me," Felicity agreed. "The trouble is, I never mean to upset people —it just happens. What's she down here for? She was in the sick bay in the Home."

"That was when they thought she was going to be a student nurse, in case your poor memory is too tired to do its work," the staff nurse reminded her. "Now she's just a stranger, she has to be treated as an ordinary patient. Get it?"

Felicity sighed. "What do they call her on her notes?"

"Miss X," she was told. "Now get moving with the BP round. I'm sure you can manage that without disaster."

"Oh, do I have to, Staff? What are the juniors doing?"

"Sterilizing gloves and doing the specimens. Don't tell me you could be trusted to do either of those jobs?"

"No, I see what you mean, Staff," Felicity said quickly, and vanished into the sluice.

It seemed a good idea to bring a whole pile of them at once, but they were hot metal, and Felicity didn't realize how hot they were until she had got half way. To her horror she couldn't go on holding them, and Alan West was approaching from the side passage. His eyebrows almost vanished to his hairline as she stood there trying to balance the swaying pile of metal BPs. She blushed to the roots of her hair and wished the wretched man would take himself away so that she could die of shame quietly out here, but he didn't go.

He just stood there, hands on hips, looking at her.

She did what seemed to be the best thing, and turned and staggered back into the sluice, just in time before the whole pile came down with a clatter that surely must be heard all over the hospital.

As the last sound died away, Felicity heard the staff nurse coming out of the ward "What on earth—?" she began, and Alan West answered, "Only Nurse Mann. She seems to be permanently set on a disaster course."

Felicity thought, "I'll never forgive him for that, not ever!" and she felt so low that she almost emulated Bridget's rash act and walked out of the hospital for good. But in Felicity's case the thought of her grandparents stopped her.

Later, much later, when she got to the bed of the girl with no memory, she heard the three talkative women patients saying things like, "There goes our parcel of trouble!"

The girl's eyes snapped open. Such brown eyes, and so steady and serious, and she said quietly, "Don't take any notice of them. They've got nothing else to do. It really is pretty grim lying in bed with time on your hands, and I expect they're used to being so busy they don't even stop to sit down."

"Thanks," Felicity said, "but you missed the point. I wouldn't mind if I were just anyone, but I'm the special target on account of being the RMO's sister. Like a queer animal brought new to the zoo, if you see what I mean."

"Because of me, do you mean?" the girl asked.

"A bit because of that, but mostly because I asked him to go to the station, anyway, and meet my friend, and she was supposed to be carrying that wretched damaged case. Identification, if you see what I mean."

"I see. I wonder why I was carrying it?"

"You must have picked it up in mistake for yours. That's what she thinks, anyway," Felicity said absently, and skidded along the polished floor to the next bed.

When she came to the girl's bed again, she said to Felicity, "What you said about your friend—have you seen her, then? I thought people were saying she was missing."

Mrs. Binny was frankly listening. Since she had been in hospital, her head pains had eased up. She had a lively curiosity and better ears than Mrs. Mobbs or Mrs. Gadd. Felicity looked wrathfully at her, and said, "Tell you later."

It was no use. The women were waiting for her. "What's been going on, duck?" Mrs. Mobbs asked frankly. "Is it really true that that good-looking brother of yours went to the station and brought back the wrong girl? There's a tale for you! What will these young men think up next?"

Felicity shut her mouth tightly.

"Leave her alone," said Mrs. Gadd. "That poor girl's had enough teasing, one way and another. Anyway, who believes anything in this place? Rare gossip-hole, I call it."

Mrs. Mobbs was astonished. She tried

to heave her weight over to look at Mrs. Gadd, but she couldn't. She lay back panting, and wheezed, "That's a good one, coming from you of all people, after you saying that the RMO's sweet on that new girl. Well, you know you did—you said that staff nurse had better look out, too."

Felicity's flaming face, as she turned away, caught the staff nurse's eye. "What is it, Nurse Mann?" she called.

Felicity didn't know what to say, and she was quite sure her face would betray her. This was truly awful. Was Maurice really interested in that girl, and showing it, too? She recalled she had thought herself that he had gone to that bedside in the sick bay rather a lot, considering the girl was a stranger and not dangerously ill.

"I'll never live down dropping those BPs," she said, and curiously enough the staff nurse was satisfied.

But during the rest of that long afternoon, Felicity kept looking at the girl as she went by, and wondering. Would Maurice be keen on her? She was certainly good-looking. In fact, Felicity had to allow, if the girl weren't looking so desperately worried, and if she had some decent make-up, she would really be rather ravishing. Those dark brown eyes and that dark hair—very nice. Poor old Staff Nurse Black wasn't much to write home about, in comparison, Felicity thought dispassionately.

Lockers was her next job. Keep me busy and out of mischief, Felicity muttered to herself. Yet it did give her the chance to chat with that girl without the three old women hearing. And without the staff nurse noticing.

"I say, do you feel ill or anything?" Felicity asked her.

"No. Perfectly fit. In fact, I'm going to ask Dr. Mann if I can get up and do something useful. I must. I can't lie here. Everyone else is so ill, it's depressing. And they won't discharge me while I can't remember anything—he said they wouldn't."

"How frightful for you. Has Dr. Corley seen you yet?"

"Yes. He asked me a lot of questions

—you know the sort of thing. One is supposed to say a certain thing by way of answer. I don't think I gave the right answers. I know I didn't give the police the right answers. '

Felicity sat back on her heels in sheer astonishment. "The police have questioned you?"

"Well, a detective. He was very nice, but I can't think what he hoped to gain. He wouldn't answer my questions."

"What did you ask him?" Felicity wanted to know.

"Things such as: did anything happen on that train. Well, Dr. Mann did say that my memory might have gone because something I'd seen worried me, but then I suppose it might have been something I'd seen in one of the places we'd passed."

"Well, that's an idea. Why don't we draw up a list of the places that train goes through and see if anything did happen there?"

"It was a slow train and stopped at masses of stations," the girl said tiredly.

Felicity said sharply, "Did someone tell you that or did you remember it?"

The girl stared at her and then looked scared. "I don't think I could possibly have remembered it. Someone must have said so."

"Nurse Mann, you've done this locker so thoroughly I wonder there's any surface left on the woodwork," the staff nurse said icily.

Felicity moved on, but she was given the teas to take round later, and that gave her another chance to speak to the girl.

"I've been thinking—" she began, but the patient said quickly, "Do you ever have a chance to go into the sick bay?"

"Not if I know it," Felicity said stoutly. "The only reason I'd get in there is to be sent to clean it for punishment, I'm too healthy. Why?"

"I think I lost something there. I wondered if anything had been found."

"What, for instance?" Felicity wanted to know.

"Never mind. Your brother—is it true he's engaged to the staff nurse?"

"Good heavens, no," said Felicity. "What a ghastly thought!"

"Is he . . . is he engaged to anyone?" she pursued.

"Not yet, and I don't want him to be. Life's difficult enough, without collecting a bossy sister-in-law on the way," said Felicity.

As she came back down the ward, however, she saw Maurice go towards that girl's bed, and her heart sank. It was true what those horrid gossiping patients were saying. And as if she needed confirmation, she saw the staff nurse glance up from a thermometer she was reading. A quick glance, but the look on her face was enough. So she had noticed Maurice's interest in that girl, too.

Felicity finished taking her trolley of cups and plates back to the kitchen, her mind in a whirl. She was embarrassed and angry. Maurice had no right to look so soppy at a patient. If it had been any other doctor, it would have been bad enough, but one's own brother! She didn't know why she was angry. She just knew she didn't like it. And that girl had been asking if he was engaged or anything!

Alan West came and stood by her. Strictly speaking, the doctors were not encouraged in this ward kitchen, and no one deplored it more than Felicity, who would have liked a brisk verbal sparring with someone like Toby Fairbairn, for instance, who was fun and a great sport. But she applauded the rule when it came to a question of Alan West, only rules didn't appear to keep him out.

"You told Matron," he accused.

She was still upset over Maurice and that girl, so she didn't choose her words. "She cornered me. I couldn't do anything else. Besides, from what she said, I got the impression you'd already told her about us."

He studied her upturned face. The innocence and youth had gone, he noticed, in astonishment. She looked rather drawn, and vaguely . . . he searched for a word and found 'disillusioned', but that surely couldn't be right?

"What's the matter?" he asked

abruptly. "Fed up because you dropped the pile of BPs?"

She shook her head, staring down at the dirty cups and saucers and jammy plates that fell to her lot to wash up. Why didn't he go, so that she could get on with the job?

"What then?" he persisted.

She shrugged. "It's been a quite horrid day, even for me. What Matron said . . ."

"Don't tell me someone's said something you really noticed, my dear?" he said lightly, but his voice was gentle.

A tear splashed down her cheek, but she didn't notice it, she was so angry, and so lost. "She egged me on to tell her about our friendship, Bridget's and mine, then she tore it to ribbons and made it seem cheap and tawdry."

"Well, your friend Bridget isn't really up to much, is she? She did run out on you last night, and that wasn't fair. You kept your part of the bargain and she hadn't even the decency to do what she promised."

"There must be a good reason," Felicity said fiercely.

"I hope so, for her sake," he told her. "She's for the high jump otherwise."

"Anyway, she was all I had," Felicity muttered. "It's not nice to have no one."

"No," he agreed, to her surprise, still in that gentle voice. "It's not nice to have no one. I know it, too."

She looked up quickly. "You do?" she said doubtfully. It occurred to him that she thought he was, in PTS language, taking the micky, so he said swiftly, "I do indeed. Isn't it possible to believe that someone as old as I am can be lonely sometimes?"

Those bright eyes of hers studied him carefully, so he went on quickly, before she could have any more doubts, "But you won't want to hear about my feelings. Let's consider your plight. You'd better try to find your friend Bridget, before her guardian comes to the hospital and makes a fuss. I daresay it isn't beyond all reason that he'll be gunning for you, as well. He might be forgiven for thinking that you two girls were cooking something up between you."

She shook her head. "I don't think I'd care if he did. I just want to be left alone."

She glared at him, daring him to say something tart about that. "You may not believe this, but I'd just like to get through one day, *one* day, without trouble. Just get through one day and feel I'd done a good job for once. But no, I can't even carry a pile of BPs without dropping them. Oh, what's the use?"

"I think there's every hope that we'll make something of you yet," he told her quietly. "If that's how you feel, then you can't be so bad. Anyway, in case you're tempted to feel sorry for yourself and say you have bad luck, I firmly believe that luck is what you make it. Just keep on trying, and don't mind if you do get a rocket for being clumsy. Sooner or later you'll find people will notice you've stopped larking about, and that's when the luck will change."

He left her then. He was quite sure she didn't know where Bridget Moore was this time. He was filled with consternation to discover that he didn't like to see her with her face all wet, and that for two pins he would have suggested helping her with that mess of washing up. What did he think he was playing at, going all soppy and protective about a PTS babe?

Later that day, the enquiry agent that the Colonel had said he would engage if they didn't find Bridget, called at the hospital. He expected to find Bridget there, of course, and when he didn't, he interviewed Felicity, in Matron's office. He got nowhere. Felicity was intimidated by Matron, after the previous interview, and she didn't want to have to say anything about Alan West and the way he had surprised them in the gardener's shed. He had been very sporting considering she had told Matron that he had known something about Bridget's turning up so late at night.

Felicity felt she would have given a lot to know how much Matron knew about the affair, and whether she had spoken to Alan West about it, and whether Maurice had had words with Matron—Matron certainly seemed much more frosty than on that other occasion.

After a lot of careful questioning, the enquiry agent got up to go. "It would appear that this young lady knows nothing," he murmured, and looked hard at Matron. Neither he nor Matron missed the relief flaring across Felicity's face.

She wasn't entirely surprised, therefore, when—released suddenly and without reason from her week's detention—Felicity went joyfully out of the hospital that night, and found the man leaning against a bus stop post, watching the gates. Waiting, she told herself indignantly, for her to lead him to where Bridget was hiding.

5

MAURICE did his rounds with no great pleasure that day. He had had an unhappy interview with Matron, about his young sister. Matron was beginning to wonder whether they were doing the best thing in keeping her at the hospital, and it all depended now on the exam. in PTS. Maurice felt that that wouldn't weigh one way or the other. Felicity had an indifferent record. Some days she got through her lessons with average ease and other days were black days so far as work was concerned. And even when she did turn out fairly good work, those days were marred by her nonsense in the classroom. She was a great disrupter of discipline, a fact which would go against her.

Then, too, there had been a telephone call from his home. The old man was ill. Not dangerously ill, but his health was not as good as it had been, and any worry now, especially about Felicity, would not really be wise. The housekeeper had been most insistent about that. The grandmother was in a very anxious state, too.

At the hospital, too, was the added anxiety about Alan West. At first Maurice had thought that Alan was just throwing in a little help, but now there was a rumour going around, connected with Felicity. Every time Maurice tried to engage Felicity in conversation she hid, and he hadn't the time to keep chasing her. West was just about as elusive, too.

Other things worried him. He wasn't very happy about Mrs. Gadd. She had been a patient on and off for a long time. Like many of the gastrics, she could have stayed at home if she had stuck to a rigid diet, but she liked her food, and she was inclined to think that a diet could be elastic; as she herself put it, a good binge today and no food at all tomorrow.

He examined her today with misgivings. She was a very sick woman.

"I expect you'll turn me over to the

surgeons, won't you, doctor?" she said sadly, as she realised he was looking much more serious than usual.

"I don't want to," he told her firmly. "I really don't want to."

Mrs. Mobbs didn't improve, either. He wondered if she realised that that enormous weight was straining her heart, and if she did ever find out, would it do any good? Or would she still persuade her relatives to bring in food, which she hid in her locker?

Mrs. Binny was very ill. There was a worrier if ever there was one. He sat by her bedside and talked gently to her.

"Who is looking after your home?"

She rolled her head fretfully from side to side. "No one, doctor, because my husband doesn't like strangers in the house, and anyway, he's used to my cooking. He wouldn't eat anything that the woman next door cooked, because she has a fag hanging at the corner of her mouth all the time and the ash drops into the pastry."

"But he could get his food out, surely?"

"Oh, no, doctor, the canteen food is all fat, frying—you know—and it upsets his stomach. Oh, can I go home?"

"Yes, when we've found out what makes the pains in your head, and taken steps to put it right. It wouldn't be sensible to go home at once and have your husband come home to that nicely cooked meal and find his wife lying on the floor in a blackout, and all the food boiling over, now would it?" He smiled as he said it, but Mrs. Binny nodded.

"Yes, I see what you mean, but how can I lie here, not knowing what he's doing, or whether they're leaving the bread, or the cat's got at the liver? It's such a worry!"

"I have a suggestion to make. Ask your husband to see the Almoner. She's full of bright ideas to put these domestic problems right. Tell him that until they're put right and you stop worrying, we won't be able to put you right, so he'll be the loser in the long run. I'm sure he'll co-operate."

"Yes, I'm sure," she said, without much conviction. "But there's something else worrying me. That poor girl in the next bed."

That claimed his attention at once. The girl he had met, not so long ago, believing her to be Bridget Moore.

"What about her?"

"Well, they've put her under now, but she's been crying, ever so quiet, under the bedclothes. And she talks in her sleep. In the middle of the night, see, when everyone else is out cold, and I'm lying here worrying myself sick wondering if my husband's got at any clothes that weren't properly aired or tried to wash out something for himself and not bothered to dry it, and I heard her distinctly say, 'I had it in the sick bay, but it's gone'. That's how she kept on. All night long."

He thanked her for telling him. "About you and your worries, Mrs. Binny. How old is your husband?"

"Five years older than I am."

"Has he ever been in the Services?"

"Oh, yes, he was in the Navy as a very young man."

"Then do stop worrying about him,

because with that background, he would have been trained to look after himself very nicely, whatever impression he may have given you. And I don't want to hear that you've been lying awake in the small hours any more." And he got up and went to the next bed.

The late sunshine slanted through the tall windows of the ward, and caught the girl's eyelashes. Dark as they were, they were tipped with gold. She really was very attractive indeed.

As he stood there looking down at her, her lids fluttered open. She lay looking at the white coat at the side of her bed, and gradually her eyes worked upwards until they found and met his.

"Hello there," he said softly. "How are you feeling?"

"Thick in the head," she said. She made a movement to sit up, and she realised where she was. White paint, yellow walls, tall windows, uncurtained, masses of flowers on chests and tables down the centre of the ward, and beds—rows and rows of them, it seemed to her, each with an occupant, mainly elderly ones. The Sibylla Stansfield Ward in St. Mary's Hospital, Uxley Green. "Do let me get up," she pleaded.

"In a few days," he promised. "We've found, at least, that you weren't sickening for anything. We had to make sure."

"I've got to get out of this ward," she fretted.

He sat down on the stool which he pulled from beneath the high bed, and felt her pulse, and while her wrist lay passively in his hand, he murmured, "Where would you go?"

She hadn't thought of that. "I don't know," she said blankly, and her pulse began to leap and race.

"Take it easy," he told her. "I've been thinking. If you don't go mad and get a high temperature," and he smiled slightly at her, "I was wondering whether you might care to take a resident job in the hospital, until you remember where you came from and where you were bound for."

She flushed. "You mean, create a job for me?"

"No, indeed I do not. I just happen to know that they're at least three short in the appointments section. You would help to reduce that, if you felt you could answer the telephone and see people's cards, get out the files and that sort of thing. It doesn't seem very difficult work to me."

Her face lit and she beamed at him. "Oh, I'd like that, if I could. I've been so scared, lying here, wondering what was to become of me. It's a horrible thought, not knowing. There might be parents some-where—only in that case they would have had a message on the radio, wouldn't they —or I might have been going to meet them or friends—only they would have gone to the police, surely?—but if I'd been on a visit, a surprise visit, for instance, then no one would have expected me—"

She looked anxious again. That very beautiful smile that had changed her face from quiet good looks to sheer beauty for a moment had faded. She was very worried again.

He nodded. His own thoughts had gone further than that. There might have been a man involved. There was nothing on her left hand, to indicate engagement or if she was married, no mark to show that a ring had ever been there, but it didn't prove anything. "Do you think if I rattled off the names of the stations that train passed through, it might help?"

"You can try," she frowned. She was ready to try anything now.

"Starting with Birmingham," he said, and he went through the long list of names she would have seen flash by, or where that train would have stopped, but it was obvious that none of them rang a bell.

"Are the police still doing anything?" she faltered. "I was thinking, I must have had a case of my own. Or else there would have been more in that handbag. One doesn't go for a whole day's trip with no more than that in a bag—unless it isn't mine, but then whose would it be?"

"What did you do with the bag?" he asked her, as casually as he could, remembering what Mrs. Binny had told him.

"I don't know. Oh, yes, when I was first sedated, I had it in the sick bay. I suppose it's there now."

"Much more likely to have been put with your clothes," he said. "I'll find out."

"I don't want to take your time up," she fretted. "But if there's someone like the Almoner who could talk it over with me—I can't just lie here and wonder who I am."

He got up to go. "I'll come back when I've done my round. Something may have occurred to me by then," he promised.

He was so preoccupied that he didn't notice Felicity on the ward, looking at him, although he had wanted to speak to her about this awful business.

He went down the ward to the next very ill person, wondering what he would say next time he went back to that girl's bed. He had already spoken to the Almoner and she hadn't any great hopes at all. As she had pointed out, it had been a full train, with people getting on and off at several stops. Also that girl hadn't been wearing anything very conspicuous, such as

135

Bridget's cream suit and green accessories. Neither was she a redhead.

What was more, the Almoner put it to him that that girl might be really on her own. A lot of girls were. She might have been going to London to an interview for a new job. "Or she might be like that accident case we had last year," the Almoner said, thinking, remembering. "The girl who had come off a liner and had her luggage left at a hotel where she stayed a couple of days, and then she thought she'd look up some old friends of her family for a surprise, without telling anyone where she was going. The accident happened to her on the way, and neither the hotel people or the old friends knew anything about that journey of hers. No roots, nothing."

"And after we'd lost her, DOT, the luggage came to light," he said harshly. He hated his patients to finish up like that, especially when Sir James Packer had done the operation. "Anyway, we haven't lost this girl, and we must find out where she came from and who she is. There must be something the police can do."

"Short of having a picture shown publicly for identification . . . but that's only in case of missing persons, with foul play suspected," the Almoner mused. "No one has claimed a relative missing, with her colouring. What more can we do?"

Later that afternoon, in Casualty, the RMO came across old Dan Kent. He had the simple happy face of a child and the nicest nature of any man the RMO knew. Dan often said he got his nice nature because his life was so restful and so peaceful, doing what he liked doing best. He was a pavement artist.

"Good gracious, that's a nasty place you've got there, Dan," said Maurice, looking at the old man's leg.

"My fault, doc. Caught it when I fell down the steps a couple of weeks ago and didn't clean it up. Turned nasty, hasn't it?"

"It certainly has. Why don't you come in for a few days? Give you a chance of a rest and some good food."

But Dan Kent wouldn't. He said he'd lose his pitch. It was the best in Uxley Green, outside the church in the main square. "Doc, everyone as comes to this town goes through King's Square," he said earnestly. "And I know the very chap as'd pinch me pitch if I'm not there."

So Maurice did what he could for the old man's leg and made him promise to come in regularly and have it cleaned up and dressed. "If you don't, you'll have to come in here, and it'll be ages before you get out again," Maurice threatened.

The old man hastily promised and escaped. "You're a toff, doc, anything I can do for you, any time, anything," he said over his shoulder, as if afraid if he stood still to make his goodbyes, he would be grabbed and warded.

Maurice smiled. He was such a nice old chap, he thought. And then the mystery girl upstairs intruded into his thoughts and he forgot about old Dan Kent.

He went back to the Sibylla Stansfield Ward, as he had promised, but he hadn't anything new to offer her by way of ideas. She had, however.

"I've been thinking," she said. "That friend of your sister's, the one you went to meet."

"Bridget Moore," he prompted her.

"Yes, well, what is she like? Her disposition, I mean. Practical joke type, or just scatterbrained?"

"Honestly, I have no idea, but I would say the latter. Why?"

"It was a thought. She might have wanted to play a practical joke on someone, and I was handy, perhaps, and that was how I happened to have the case. What do you think of that for an idea?"

"It could be, only I don't quite see where it gets us," he was bound to point out.

"Yes, you see, in that case, she would have singled me out and would presumably remember me by sight and it might just be possible that she would remember which station I boarded the train at, don't you see? And what happened to my own luggage—or perhaps she might remember seeing a name on my case?"

"It's an idea," he agreed. "But one that won't work, I'm afraid."

"But why, Dr. Mann? I know she was found—your sister said so. Can't your sister ask her, if you can't find it convenient to do such a tiresome job?"

"I'd do it with the greatest of pleasure —I want to speak to that young lady myself—but it so happens it isn't possible. She certainly turned up last night, but she's gone again. Apparently she's in trouble on her own account, and won't face her guardian, if he turns up at the hospital."

Privately Maurice hoped that the Colonel wouldn't find it either possible or worthwhile to come in person to the hospital, but he did. Maurice had to see him.

Alan West couldn't be found, but between them Matron and Maurice cooled the Colonel down and promised to let him know the minute that Bridget was found.

The Colonel wasn't satisfied. "It's your

young sister I really want to see, sir! And I don't intend to leave Uxley Green until I do."

Felicity couldn't be found, either. She had by then gone out. She was in a very angry mood and the thought of the private detective engaged by the Colonel trailing her like this brought a flicker of interest to life. She decided to give him a run for his money.

Uxley Green was always an interesting place to the young nurses. Felicity walked along the bank of the river and stopped at a gap in the hedge and whistled as if it were a signal. The detective wasn't far behind. Felicity joyously wriggled through the hedge and hid there. He came bursting through and began to jog-trot through the copse, while Felicity slithered back through the hedge and on to the river path again. He was very cross when he realised she had tricked him.

He found her later, leaning on a wall, admiring some ducks in a small pond, but she got away just before he reached her and nipped on to a bus that was just pulling out. This was the sort of hide and seek game she and Bridget had been so adept at, in the hectic schooldays they hadn't long left behind. She got off the bus at the next stop and doubled back in time to see the detective running for it, taking a flying leap that almost brought disaster. The conductor said a few things to him as he hauled him aboard.

In some measure, Felicity got back some of her good humour and self-confidence during that chase. She led the detective into a dark and dingy shop that was ambitiously labelled 'antiques' but which held the dirtiest, smelliest load of junk imaginable, including old clothes. Felicity knew the man and went out through the back of the shop into a yard. The next time the detective found her, she was pensively staring at Dan Kent's artistic efforts on the pavement. But here she came to grief. Staring up at her from the paving stones, in full blazing crude colour, was Bridget's face, the red hair replaced by corn yellow, a vivid colour which didn't suit Bridget at all.

Dan Kent said softly, "Does your brother know you're here, miss?" And he winked.

"Never you mind," she said wrathfully. "What made you do that ghastly picture?"

"Oh, that one? The young lady insisted. And she promised me five bob if I was to see you and give a message where to meet her. She's give me five bob already for doing that."

"Did she? Well, how did she know I've got five bob? It's near the end of the month, too."

"She said you'd find five bob, miss, you wanted to know that bad," he grinned.

"All right, here you are. Now, where is she?"

"In the crypt, miss, just behind us."

Felicity nodded, belatedly looked round, but couldn't see the detective anywhere, and hurried into the crypt of the old church. She didn't think it likely that the detective would use his brains, since he had let her trick him time and time again during the afternoon, but he had got tired of Felicity's tricks that afternoon, and he had had the forethought to take off and carry his light raincoat, and disguise his face to a certain extent by wearing sun-glasses. Felicity had passed him over, looking for the man who had been chasing her for the last hour.

Bridget was sitting disconsolately on a stone seat in the crypt. It was cold down there. She wasn't happy with the new blonde hair, and after paying so much for one item, she now found herself short of cash. Felicity couldn't help her.

"Why don't you come back to the hospital with me, you clot?" Felicity expostulated. "You'll be in awful trouble if you don't."

"I'll be in worse trouble if I do," Bridget said clearly. "I remembered after I legged it from your Dr. West that I hadn't told you what else happened on that train—before it drew into Latchmarket, I mean."

"Not more trouble?" Felicity gasped.

"What's the matter with you? You used to like japes and this was a gorgeous jape. Listen, this fellow I was telling you about, this Claude Langley, he got a bit insistent about the Thing—"

"Yes, you said that," Felicity reminded her.

"Well, I thought I'd give him a run for his money, so I hid it, but I let him see me wrapping something up in a paper bag. It was actually only my old manicure case, but it was about the same size, and it fooled him. He chased me through to the luggage department and there was a lot of priceless stuff in there belonging to a conjuror, you know the sort of thing— disappearing boxes—well, a sort of wardrobe you step in and vanish."

Felicity was aware that for the first time she no longer found this sort of recital funny. She said so. "We've got big trouble on our hands here, and all you can yatter about is larking with some conjuror's props in the luggage van—and how on earth was it the guard didn't discover you?"

"What's got into you? You used to find this killing! Like I'm telling you, the guard *did* come, and Claude Langley hid and so did I, only I went into the beastly cupboard. I don't know how it worked or how I got out, but I did, after the guard had gone."

"Well, what happened about this new boy-friend of yours? I suppose you've been home with his family—you'd have the cheek for even that," Felicity said in disgust.

"No, I haven't. He's no boy-friend of mine. He's just a common thief. He wanted that Thing and he was going to have it. The thing is, he pinched the manicure set after all. It was a sort of scrum, in and out of the props, and I don't remember him taking it. He terrified me. Anyway, he tried to pull the communication cord, only it wouldn't work, but the train slowed down going round a bend and he jumped out with the booty. It was pretty grim. He took a flying leap and rolled down the embankment. I don't suppose he came to any harm, mind you, because it was all sort of soft earth and bracken and stuff, but it shook me, I can tell you. I mean, suppose it had been that

Thing the American was going to pay all that much for—?"

"Well, it wasn't, so what are you worrying about? All you've got to do is to go to the police and tell them you stuffed it down between the upholstery of the seats. It's probably there now," Felicity said crossly. Gone was the old interest in Bridget's resourcefulness, although she herself had been practising the old game this afternoon. But that had been to shake off someone pursuing her, not to protect something she had stolen!

"You don't seem to understand," Bridget gasped. "I can't do that. The guardian doesn't want it to come out. Don't you see? Someone will find it and keep it if it gets out it has any value. You know what stinkers people are."

"It's natural," Felicity said crossly. "Anyway, it must have been insured."

"No, that's the whole point. I mean, how can you insure a thing that hasn't got any special value?"

"Of course you can. Well, it could have

been insured for *something*. I suppose your guardian didn't pinch it?"

Bridget was quite unfairly shocked. Felicity would have thought she'd laugh, but that didn't strike her as being funny. They both seemed to have drifted away from each other over this business. "Of course he wouldn't pinch anything. Neither would I. I just borrowed it, and don't suggest he's borrowed it or taken it or anything. It belongs to him—"

"Where did he get it in the first place?" Felicity asked.

"I don't know. Found it out East, I suppose, or else bought it for a bottle of Scotch or a string of beads."

Felicity's scornful look penetrated and Bridget blushed. "Well, that's the way people pick up things to sell for a big price. It's the done thing. You have to be smart enough to see what someone will want to buy from you, and anyway, the guardian braved all sorts of dangers that his American customer probably wouldn't care to brave. The thing is, and what I wanted you for, was to get a bit of a letter back for me. I lost that on the train, too, only in a different place. I just think that girl might have picked it up."

"What girl?" Felicity asked, very much on the alert now.

"That girl your brother met. Lesley Something—oh, I remember—Lesley Weldon."

"*You know her*?" Felicity asked, in horror.

"What's the matter with you? Of course I don't know her. You clot, you're all different today—what's got into you?"

"You know her name, yet you know everyone's going mad to find out who she is—" Felicity stormed.

"Shut up, you'll get us thrown out," Bridget grumbled. "I don't remember anyone asking me what her name was."

"You know she's lost her memory."

"Well, what about it? I can't make it come back, can I? And anyway, I'm only guessing her name's Lesley Weldon because that was on the case she had by her feet. It might have been someone else's case she was using."

"How did you know?" Felicity pursued. "I thought you said you didn't know what had happened to my case?"

"You don't listen to me," Bridget complained. "I came back to find it in my compartment, because your case marked the spot where I'd put the Thing, only it was gone. I searched the compartments for a few minutes, but the train would be going, so I got off and I saw this girl walking off with the case and then she fell flat on her face. And your big brother emerged from hiding."

"Why didn't you speak to him?" Felicity exploded.

"What for? I'd have got lugged back to the hospital, wouldn't I, and I didn't want to go, did I? I told you all that."

"Christmas, it gets worse," Felicity muttered. "Well, where *is* the case with her name on it, or is that asking too much?"

"I stashed it away in the station left luggage," Bridget said in a surly voice. "And in case you think I'm going to cough up the ticket, let me say here and now, without any fear for the consequences, that I've lost it."

And at that interesting point, the man in the sunglasses came down and said pleasantly that he had heard all that, and that he had a few things to ask them, and that they'd better go back to the hospital with him because he was the private detective the Colonel had hired to find Bridget.

6

IT was soon all over the hospital. Felicity could never understand how the grapevine worked. Who could have got hold of the story? And how?

They were taken by the detective, in a taxi, back to the hospital, straight to Matron, and there they found the irate Colonel, and Maurice, and even Alan West, who had been found in the meantime and had told Matron about the escapade that night.

Matron was furious with him, of course. "Really, Dr. West, I should have thought a responsible person like yourself would have come to me straight away!"

He cocked an amused and rather satirical eyebrow at her. "*Would* you, Matron? Come now, what sort of idiot would it have made me look? I'm telling you now only because circumstances seem to indicate that it wouldn't be wise to sit on the information any longer, but I don't pretend I like it. Our friend Dr. Mann seems to find it rather amusing, too, but he may find himself at the wrong end of his young sister's sense of humour one of these days. I can't say I shall sympathise much with him!"

One person who did thoroughly sympathise with Dr. West, however, was Colonel Partridge. "You've only had the brunt of Dr. Mann's young sister's sense of fun, sir!" he growled. "I live in fear of my ward's sense of fun. Believe me, it's no joke! Surely, Matron, you will not take the girl on here now?"

"Well, it rather depends on you, Colonel, doesn't it, and whether we find her!"

"Yes, I know," he agreed. "But I've got a good man on the job. He should track her down. The trouble is, if you don't keep her under your able eye, who *will* take her? I can't have her at home, with my wife's present state of health to consider. She needs to be kept on a chain, like an undisciplined dog—"

That shocked them all, and in the silence that followed they heard voices outside, and the detective and the two girls were announced. They had been brought straight in from the taxi, yet later, after the rocket of all rockets from Matron, the Colonel, Dr. Mann and Dr. West, the two girls found themselves dismissed to go to Home Sister, in a chastened mood, with many curious eyes following them.

As an afterthought, Matron had sent her assistant to see they reached Home Sister safely until it was decided what to do with them so they couldn't talk, but each of them was wondering what would happen to them now.

Home Sister had been briefed on the telephone, in a few short sentences while they made the journey from Matron's office to the Nurses' Home. She said tartly, "So this is Bridget Moore!" and by her expression she expected no more than double the trouble she got already from Felicity. "And you knew all the time who that poor girl was and you never came forward to say!"

Felicity's eyes widened. Matron hadn't wasted much time in spreading the glad news! At a later date she saw how the grapevine had got the story—via the telephone switchboard. The head porter hadn't been on, and the other man was young, garrulous, and inclined to brief his girl-friend, the fourth-floor maid in the Nurses' Home, as to what was happening everywhere else, particularly if it concerned the young nurses.

"Oh, no, Sister, she didn't," Felicity couldn't resist saying quickly. "She only saw the name on the other piece of luggage and assumed that that was the patient's name, but we don't know any more about the patient."

"Hasn't Miss Moore got a tongue?" Home Sister asked tartly.

So Bridget endorsed that piece of information and then they were sent up to Felicity's room. The acrobatic Linda Howland was put into another room, leaving the two quiet studious ones—Ann Taylor and Kathy Milburn—to damp down the ardour of the other two.

They were down in the classroom when Felicity and Bridget pelted up the stairs. Felicity sat down on her bed and said to Bridget, "I'll make some tea in a minute, but first of all, let's take stock of our position. Your guardian doesn't know about the Thing yet, does he? Why didn't you tell him and get it off your conscience?"

Bridget scowled. "Let him stew a bit longer," she said mutinously. "He hates me and I hate him, and I hope the Thing never turns up—and I hope it gets around among the rich Americans that my guardian isn't to be relied upon to cough up the goods!"

"Oh, I say, that's a bit steep!" Felicity protested. "You can't go on like that!"

"I could and I would, only I don't specially want to get you into trouble."

"What's more to the point," Felicity said slowly, and with belated prickings of conscience, "it might do a whole lot of harm to my brother's career if this thing boils up. I don't want people to say good-ness, that ghastly doctor has got a frightful sister who makes friends with people who pinch things. All right, you say you only borrowed it, but who's going to believe that? If you want my honest opinion, I think we ought to tell someone about the Thing before the trail gets cold. It might still be in the crack of the seat where you put it, but supposing some frightful little kid starts poking about and finds it and trades it for foreign stamps or something? It'll be lost for ever."

"I should worry," Bridget growled.

"And mud sticks," Felicity continued. "For ever afterwards people might wonder if I'd had a hand in it, or worse, they might think my brother had something to do with it. So, chum, if you don't own up, then I'm going to."

"But I told you in confidence!" Bridget wailed.

"I know that," Felicity said sturdily. "And I know you're going to say that if I do, you won't be friends with me any more. Well, let me say here and now that I don't think I'm going to be friends with you any more anyway, if you don't come clean yourself—not only about the Thing but about everything else, every little detail."

Bridget's mouth dropped open. "You must have gone round the bend, to talk like that! We always stuck together—this isn't a more awful jape than any of the others! It must be this hospital. Crikey, they brainwash you. I'm getting out here, but quick."

"You can please yourself," Felicity shocked herself by saying. "And it's not the hospital at all—I think, if I had to say what caused it, it's because everyone looks so scornfully at me. They've all got much more important things to do than to put up with people like us fooling about. And then there's that girl—Lesley Weldon—lying there. It must be absolutely hideous not to know who you are, and not to have anyone at all to turn to."

Bridget shrugged. "I've done her a good turn by telling everyone about her name. All they've got to do is to find out where she came from. Well, once you've got the name of a person—"

"But you said yourself that you don't know if it *is* her name! No, it won't do, Bridget. Either you stop your clowning and grow up, or else we part. That girl made me feel all sorts of a worm, although she was very decent and didn't say anything. But I just don't want that sort of thing to happen again. Besides—"

She broke off, furious with herself. She had almost let it pop out that Dr. West looked as if he despised her too, at times, and she liked that least of all.

"Besides what?" Bridget asked, interested.

"Besides, I've just discovered something," Felicity said, searching round in her mind for some excuse to cover up her slip, and to her great surprise finding one that happened to be the truth. "But you won't believe me. I've discovered I actually like the work here."

"Now I know you're round the bend!" Bridget sighed, flinging herself flat on her back, and pronouncing the bed to be disgustingly hard. "If you can look me in the eye and tell me you like all that stuff

—that hygiene and biology and domestic cleaning and cooking and all the other tripe you've been putting in your letters —goodness, we worked overtime to avoid things like that at school! Anyway, you're completely batty if you mean it."

"All right, I'm batty, but I really enjoyed that last time on the ward. Yes, I did! The old girls are a perfect bind and one's hands look red and rough and awful, but . . . well, I don't know. It feels like belonging to a big family. The staff all stick together and help each other, if you don't fool about, and there's a purpose behind it all. Yes, there is—I've just discovered that."

Bridget was terribly shocked. More shocked at this admission than at any other of the things that Felicity had said. Finally she stood up and said curtly, "All right, you'd better show me where to go and who to contact, and I'll tell 'em everything. And it's not because I want your beastly lukewarm friendship. It's just that I don't like being classed as a horrible worm, when I've only been doing the things that you seemed to admire so much, not so long ago."

St. Mary's, between grappling with emergencies and coping with half the accident cases that should have been sent to Wilmington, found time to listen delightedly to the rumours that flew around about Dr. Mann's young sister and that friend of hers. They heard of the row between Colonel Partridge and his ward when he heard about the treasure and of how Bridget had lost it. It was searched for, but of course, there was too big a time lapse and there was no sign of it, and he still wouldn't permit the publicity that advertising for it would bring.

They heard, too, that Bridget (under pressure) found the cloakroom ticket for the case belonging to Lesley Weldon and then lost it again, and that Matron was in such a boiling rage about Bridget that no one was anxious to cross her path for some days. And they heard, too, that Bridget coldly settled into the PTS and proceeded to make up for lost time by almost catching up the others in some subjects.

Ann Taylor was almost weeping over it. "It doesn't seem fair!" she exploded. "I've been working late at night to keep up and do well in the exams, and that girl—that scatterbrained girl who's too rich to ever need to work at all—finds she has the sort of memory that soaks facts and figures up like blotting paper. Without effort!"

Kathy Milburn was filled with despair. "I know, it's the without-effort bit that makes me wretched, too," she admitted. "But that girl isn't rich now, you know. I heard she'd lost all her money."

"Well, her guardian's rich, isn't he, so it's the same thing," Ann Taylor, from an industrial town and a small home in a mean street, exploded. "What good will she be to a sick patient? She hates slopping about in the sluice, and she loathes the thought of a BP round!"

Bridget was not only out of favour with those two. She wasn't pleasing Felicity much, either, since she had managed to attract Toby Fairbairn.

To Felicity, Bridget's new blonde dyed hair was terrible, but to Toby it was

162

unusual, rich, fascinating, every appealing description he could think of, and with Toby, Bridget wasn't the same as she was to other people. Sister Tutor saw her as a young woman with malice-filled eyes, who escaped any practical task possible, especially if it was of the slopping water kind, but who arrogantly remembered facts and figures, and lounged about while her fellow class members struggled. To Home Sister she was still the menace she had always been before they even met her; in Home Sister's opinion the guiding factor in Felicity's own bad record, and even though Bridget was purposely quiet and apparently on her best behaviour, to Home Sister this was even more a menace, because of the emotions that lurked in that girl's brilliant eyes. A young woman Home Sister didn't feel would prove of any comfort to the patients.

But to Toby Fairbairn, Bridget was fascinating. She had the sense to keep quiet when she was with him and he told her all about himself, and how he talked! He let her know that there was big money in his family, which appeased Bridget to the extent of seeing a way clear in the near future to free herself from her guardian. His guardianship was due to finish on her marriage, and so far she hadn't managed to meet a young man who had even as much money as she had. Now she was hard up it was a different matter.

Felicity didn't realise this. She thought Bridget was snatching at any friendship with anyone's man provided he would take her away from the hospital precincts in her precious free time. She and Felicity were rapidly drifting apart now, especially as Felicity had been put on extra ward duty to split the two up. Felicity was showing possibilities which Matron and the Ward Sisters were quick to notice. She still dropped things and made mistakes, but she was trying so hard, and apparently liking being on the wards so much. She had forgotten that Dr. West had told her how much easier life would be for her if she could manage to work up an interest in her duties. She hadn't believed it and it didn't occur to her to think over any of the things he had said to her, and he was keeping out of her way for the time being, until he saw how things developed.

It was a brilliantly sunny day when he did run into Felicity again. She was going across from the hospital to the Nurses' Home, a scowl on her lovely baby face, her shoulders hunched disconsolately. Bridget had gone off for the rest of the day in Toby's new car, a lilac shade that was easily recognisable to everyone. Alan West had seen it, too, and wondered. The grapevine hadn't fallen down on its duty and he knew all about Felicity having a growing liking for Toby.

He stopped in front of Felicity. "Oh, dear, you look as if you hate everyone, this lovely day. Do you?"

She looked up at him with no great liking, and shrugged. "My best friend has gone off with a man I rather liked, but what's that little thing?"

"So you've nothing to do? I suppose I couldn't prevail upon you to do a service for someone, then?"

"We're not allowed to go running

errands for the patients any more," she said quickly. "The Almoner doesn't like it."

"I didn't say that was what I wanted you to do," he said mildly. "It was something for a very old friend of mine, and I happen to know you have a grandmother, so I just thought it might have given you a little knowledge of what an old lady likes. My old friend is seventy-five and very rich and she seems to have everything, but I would like to send her a little something to celebrate her birthday."

As always, Felicity regarded him with cold suspicion, but was honest enough to add, "Yes, all right, and I'd better look for something for my grandmother, too. Her birthday is coming up in a couple of weeks. My grandfather as well—he's not well. Where were you going, Dr. West? Just to the local shops?"

"Actually to Wilmington, if that pleases you."

She brightened, against her will. "I've never been to Wilmington yet," she admitted.

"Then for heaven's sake go and fling on something cheerful, and don't be all day. I'll get rid of this white coat and bring the car round to the front. Race you!"

She looked after his long striding figure, in shocked amazement. Had she imagined it, or had Dr. West invited her to *race* him?

She went and changed with commendable speed into a rather nice light blue dress and matching coat, with reptile skin shoes and matching handbag. She was very good to look at, and he was pleased with her, but he knew better than to let her know it. "Hop in," he said briefly.

Maurice, standing at the corner of the X-ray department, waiting for Lesley Weldon to come out, saw them go and felt as bothered as he had on that other occasion. What was Alan West up to? Maurice had always felt a kind of desperate anxiety for his young sister, and an unrecognised tenderness, because the poor kid hadn't had any parental affection, only a fussing over by the grandparents and a lot of discipline without love at her

167

various schools. What could Alan West have to give her?

Lesley Weldon came out and followed his glance. The big car was waiting to ease out into the mainstream of traffic. She could see Felicity's bright head and Alan West's dark one, even at this distance, because the sun was shining right into the car. "What's the matter?" she asked Maurice quietly.

"My young sister, with Dr. West," he said briefly.

"She likes him very much. Do you mind? Don't tell her I said so, because she doesn't know it yet."

Maurice looked at her in amazement, the tender look that was always there fighting to be uppermost. "What does that mean, for heaven's sake?"

"Felicity hasn't been very happy, and she clashes with Dr. West, but I think it's just the first round, you know. She'll finish up being devoted to him. He likes her very much, too."

"Am I supposed to believe that they

both confided in you?" he asked gently, laughing softly at her.

"Maurice, you won't believe this, but I watched them, through half closed eyes, when I was lying so long in that ward, wondering who I was till I felt sick about it. It was an escape measure to watch other people. One can learn a lot by unobtrusively observing them. I used to watch you, too."

He flushed and took her arm. "Come on, what about that walk, or other people will be watching both of us. We're in full view of all the windows."

They walked sedately, a yard apart, out of the hospital and down the road to the passages leading from street to busy street, riverwards. Once they had reached the cool green shades, and the traffic was no more than the hum of an angry insect, in the distance behind them, he took her arm again. "Isn't this nice, this river? Right bang in the middle of shabby grey old Uxley Green? I just can't think how we'd manage without it."

"It is nice," she agreed, but her eyes were shadowed.

"Can't you let it slide into the background for a while, that problem of yours, and relax in the sunshine?" he asked her.

She shook her head. "No. Can't seem to get rid of it. You don't expect me to, do you? Not really? All these weeks, and here we are, no further forward with discovering who I am, even though we have my name."

"Yes, if dear Bridget Moore hadn't lost the cloakroom ticket, we might have found the answer in your case."

"Do you really believe she has lost it?" Lesley said suddenly. "I mean, although that sounds uncharitable, it also sounds to me as improbable, the thought that she could lose something so important, and yet have such a mind for soaking up facts and figures."

"Unless to her it was supremely unimportant," he said quietly. "Anything she wants to remember, that girl will remember. She obviously wants to make a big splash showing off her wonderful memory in the PTS, but keeping an eye on things and their safety doesn't rank among the important things to her. Selfish brat, that girl."

"But isn't it ridiculous? Someone must know me. I must have been going somewhere. And how is it the police couldn't discover that case?"

"That puzzles me. But remember that she couldn't recall (or so she says) just which cloakroom she took it to. She wandered about between tea-time and almost midnight. She took cabs here and there, too. She might have left it at any one of five main stations."

"But I would have thought the police would have just opened up all the cases—" she began.

"I don't think that would help, in this particular circumstance, would it?" he said gently. "You would be there, and what would happen when they opened the various cases? You wouldn't be able to remember what belonged to you."

"Oh, no, I'd forgotten." She put a hand to her head. "I get so impatient. Impatient in the oddest circumstances. For instance, that good-looking houseman, Toby Fairbairn . . ."

"Oh, dear, the one my sister appears to have lost to her very dear friend Bridget," Maurice murmured wryly. It worried him. It wasn't fair. Bridget had no business to take Toby away like that. Felicity was no flirt; he was the only young man in the hospital that she had really liked, so far as he knew, and he thought he knew his sister pretty well.

Lesley was still talking. "There he was, fiddling with the drip-stand, and I nearly said something. I shocked myself. I nearly told him how to do it. What did I know about it? I shut my mouth tightly and shut my eyes too, and willed myself to think of something else, then the staff nurse came along and fiddled with it and between them they got it to go. Now why do you suppose I get so irritable about things that really don't concern me?"

"It's natural, my dear. I do understand how you feel. You may not know this, but I lost my own memory for a day—one day only—when I got hit on the head with a cricket ball. The memory of those twelve hours can still give me the creeps."

"And your memory came back?"

"Oh, well, yes, it was rather different. I was concussed, and several bones broken, because I lost my balance in falling and went down the bank. We were playing away from home and I didn't know the pitfalls. There was a stream at the boundary, at a much lower level, and a tangle of tree trunks, undergrowth, big stones and rubbish—oh, I was in quite a mess by the time I was hauled up, and out of action for some time, but thank heavens only a few hours before I remembered who and where I was!"

She shivered. "Have you got a complex about water, since then?"

He chuckled. "No. I never get complexes about anything. I'm not superstitious, and I don't have to have a light on in my room at night."

"You're laughing at me! No, it was a silly question. I'm sure you're the least likely person to get the willies over anything. Can you tell me this: is it within reason that I should get that feeling—well, the old gossips on Sibylla Stansfield Ward are always saying, 'it's on the tip of my tongue', but the thing eludes them in the end. And that's the sort of feeling I get— so nearly remembering, and then not quite. It scares me rather."

"Don't let it. I assure you, it's all right. One day something may happen to make your memory come back. It won't be pleasant, but when it does happen, your troubles will all be over, I promise you."

"Will they? I wonder. I wish, oh, how I wish it could happen. I want to know if I have anyone belonging to me. It's a terrible lonely feeling when the other patients get visitors—families, friends, neighbours—and there isn't anyone for me. There must be someone!"

"I hope there isn't," he said in a low fierce tone. As she shot up her head to look at him, her dark brown eyes wide with surprise, he said hastily, "Oh, I shouldn't have said that! It isn't ethical, to say the least, and I shouldn't have said it, but I meant it! There's nothing much I can do about it. I just hope, passionately hope, that there isn't anyone in your life."

"But you can't say that," she whispered. "You don't know anything about me! Not anything!"

"I know you, as you are. I've seen you, helped you, through some pretty trying circumstances, and I liked the way you reacted. That's good enough for me."

"Maurice!" she whispered. "I wish I could say—"

"What? Say what, my dear?"

"I wish I could think that I had the right to say what I feel about it. But I can't get rid of the feeling that I might just like you tremendously *now*, and that when my memory comes back (if it does!) I might be remembering someone else and that person would blot you out and I'd wonder how I could ever have forgotten him and cared for you. Do you understand?"

"Yes, I understand," he said huskily. "It's a risk I have to take, because I know I care for you. There's been no one else in my life, and there never will be. I'm that sort of person."

He hesitated, then drew her to him and kissed her, very gently, on her mouth. He had wanted so much to do that, ever since he had first held her in his arms, so helpless she had been, on the station at Latchmarket that day. He held his breath as he kissed her, but she didn't shy from it. She didn't return his kiss, it was true, but she didn't appear to dislike it.

"Maurice, you're such a nice person," she whispered, drawing away from him. "I hate not to know anything about me. I'd love to feel free to—Oh, Maurice, do you see what I'm trying to say? I can't remember a thing, and yet there are times when I find myself looking at that bare finger on my left hand and feeling an odd sensation that talk of marriage was a feature in my life. My marriage? Or a wedding I was to go to? Well, I don't know. I somehow can't feel that I was always alone. It's a hideous sensation."

She felt so near tears, she turned her back on him. There was no sound, only the soft lap-lap of the water, the bird calls all around them, the soft whirring of insects, and further away, the cries of some children at play above the bridge. Maurice put his hands on her shoulders and gently turned her round. "Don't worry about it. Lean on me, till you feel you can stand on your own two feet again. I hate to be trite, but there's a certain amount of comfort in the old saying that one's fears for the future are always more hideous than the future itself when it arrives."

He tilted her chin, and this time as he kissed her, she returned his kiss. For an agonising moment they clung together. She felt that if she let go of him she would break down and never stop crying, never stop shivering for fear of the future which she felt would be coming towards her in great galloping strides at any moment now.

And then the children left the bridge and came running towards them and there was no more privacy, no more sweet intimate moments that were giving her strength and a measure of confidence which she had been wanting so much. They sprang apart and walked with a semblance of casualness along the river bank, but Maurice Mann was filled with a turbulence and a sense of unhappiness and defeat no less than hers.

He, too, feared the future in spite of all he had said by way of comfort to her. There was something hidden that they wouldn't like when it came out, he was sure. Amnesia didn't come for nothing.

Alan West, in his car with Felicity, was thinking on the same lines. "I can't tell you what causes amnesia, my dear," he said in answer to Felicity's urgent question. "I could, and probably will in the near future, give you and your friends a long and perhaps dreary lecture on the subject. But will it answer what you want to know about our mystery patient, I wonder? And would it have the same interest for you, if your brother didn't happen to like her rather a lot?"

Felicity looked fussed. "That's the whole point. I want my brother Maurice to be happy. I know I do. Yet I keep finding myself trying to invent things to stop him from seeing her because I'm scared to the marrow that something perfectly frightful will come out when she does get her memory back. Or perhaps someone will turn up one day who knows her. Won't that be horrible?"

"Oh, don't be a silly brat," he said tenderly. "How could such a thing happen?"

"I'm not supposed to be an imaginative person, but I get awful nightmares of her in the appointments section going to the glass window and pulling it back and asking some awful old woman what she wants—"

"—which I believe is her job in life at the moment, and a job which Miss Weldon herself seems to be very thankful to have," Alan said lightly.

"—and the old woman saying in a cracked voice that she was Miss Weldon's grannie or something, and they would be criminals or ex-prisoners or something perfectly ghastly, and she would burst into tears and when she saw my brother coming she'd run right out of the hospital—"

"—into the road and get run over," he finished. "That was the theme of the film at the Palace last week, if my hearing of the conversation of three nurses marching along in front of me tells me rightly," he said savagely. "Stop giving yourself the jim-jams, Felicity, or I shall shake you or —or something much worse. Come on, let's get out. We're in Wilmington, which you wanted to see so badly, and you haven't even been looking at the scenery!"

Felicity got out, grumbling gently, "I don't see any scenery, it's just a grey town like Uxley Green," and she sounded so disappointed that he squeezed her arm and said, "Shut up or you'll be bawling any minute. Come and have some coffee and slushy cream cakes at a little place I know, then we'll have a look round the shops, some food at another place I know, and then anything else you'd like to do, before we have to go back. Cheer up!"

It turned out to be the most pleasant day Felicity had remembered for a long time. Alan West's old lady might have everything, and be very rich, but Felicity averred firmly that she wouldn't have any of the things they found in the dark little junk shop under the arch near the ruins of the castle. It wasn't a gift shop. In fact, Felicity said, in much too loud a tone, that to judge by the darkness of the shop, the jumble of the goods and the absence of anyone to serve, it didn't seem as if they wanted to sell anything. Then a pleasant middle-aged man came out of the shadows and asked if he could help them, and proceeded to disentangle from the mounds of goods, things like the carved wooden snuff-box that Felicity fell in love with, and the music-box which had a block, a victim and an axe-man on the top, and when the music played 'here comes the chopper to chop off your head' from the old nursery rhyme, the little axe-man uncertainly heaved down his little axe to within a quarter of an inch of the bandaged victim's head.

"Gruesome little brute, aren't you?" Alan murmured fondly. "Want it?"

Felicity missed the warmth in his tone, and nodded her head. "Yes, I simply must have it! Not for myself, though. I was thinking of my grandfather. It might cheer him up, it's so gorgeously funny. He used to collect music-boxes. He hasn't for such a long time. I wonder why? He had a lovely painted porcelain one that I knocked down when I was little. I thought he was going to skin me, but he just looked sadly at all the pieces and he said—oh, what a funny thing, I've just remembered! After all these years, I've never thought of it until now."

"What did he say?" Alan prompted gently.

"He said something quite odd about me being such a clumsy child, I'd really have to learn not to break things in case I broke someone's heart when I grew up. What a daft thing to say to a child!" she finished crossly, and turned away with a sniff. But she came back presently, with another treasure she'd found, and which Alan bought for his old lady: a biscuit box which, when the catch was pressed to open the lid, a dancing couple on top performed a few steps and curtseyed before the lid slid sideways to open. "She likes a biscuit in the small hours when she can't sleep," he said, and looked pleased because Felicity had found it.

Before they left the shop, Felicity found something for her grandmother, too—a little box covered in odd shaped and coloured shells. "She can keep her thimbles in it," Felicity said happily.

Alan hadn't got the heart to tell her that the shells had probably been dyed those improbable colours. It was a pretty thing and she was buying it with love for her grandmother. He had never seen such warmth and affection in a young face before, and he was aware suddenly that the man in the shop was staring at them both with a lively appreciation of the first signs of budding romance. Alan could cheerfully have kicked him. Again he reminded himself that he had no right to be feeling silly over a PTS baby, and that Maurice Mann would probably not like it at all. But he couldn't resist Felicity. She was so sweet.

"You like little boxes, don't you?" he said, and looked round for the snuff-box that had taken her eye. The shop man anticipated his movement, and found it, holding it up with raised eyebrows. Alan nodded to him.

Felicity reddened to the hairline when she realised he was buying it for her. "What for?" she demanded truculently.

The shop man had left them to go and wrap the things up at the back in the shadows.

"Let's say it's to gratify a whim of mine," Alan said awkwardly.

"Lumme," she said inelegantly. "You're like any other grown-up I've ever known—you don't want to answer, so you say something all wrapped up in fancy language that doesn't mean anything!"

"Am I so grown-up?" he said painfully, frowning.

She coloured again. "You bring out the worst in me," she grumbled. "That was rude, and I apologise. Oh, I don't know how old you are—at least, common sense tells me what age you must be at the absolute least, to have got to where you are up the hospital ladder, but at times you seem quite young and good fun, like today. But you're not all that young," she amended, struggling to be truthful. "I mean, you're all full of confidence. You're never uncertain with me, like the boys I know. They're easy to handle."

"And I'm not?" He smiled broadly. "Perhaps it's as well, or you'd make mincemeat of me. The thought terrifies me!"

"Now you're laughing at me! And you haven't said why you bought me that snuff-box."

"Well, let's say that I made a bet with myself, that there were hidden depths in you. I hate to prove myself wrong to myself and when I don't (as now, because you're doing very nicely, they tell me!) then I feel I have to reward myself, so I gave myself the pleasure of buying the snuff-box for you. What do you want it for?"

"Oh, for itself. Something I really liked," she said. But she didn't say thank you for it. She was suddenly shy of him, uncertain, almost afraid of him, or of herself for this new upset feeling that was taking possession of her. She was just anxious to get out of the place, back to the familiar ground of the Nurses' Home, and people she wasn't upset with.

But when she did get back, instead of being able to go and get a quiet bath and think about today and Alan West, Felicity was confronted by Bridget.

Bridget appeared to forget that they were drifting apart. She approached Felicity much as she had done when they were at school together. The familiar pattern formed with every word, every look, from Bridget, Felicity thought.

"Fel, the most ghastly thing's happened!" she began.

And as of old, Felicity said, by habit almost, "Tell me while I fling my clothes off and get into something comfy."

It now no longer mattered that Bridget had taken Toby Fairbairn. Toby was a pleasant boy that Felicity could handle. He never made her feel so peculiar and he had never bought her anything, or given her a day like today which was suddenly, in retrospect and the safety of the Nurses' Home, rather sweet and precious.

Bridget said, "Toby and I came back and were saying goodbye and all that, and I found that ticket in my coat pocket. Well, it was the coat I was wearing the day I took her beastly case to the cloakroom. It wasn't a station cloakroom at all—it was the cloakroom of the hotel where I had dinner. I was fed-up with carrying it about by then and I'd almost left it in one taxi, so I thought I'd drop it there. Then I forgot to bring it away."

"How can you forget a thing like that?" Felicity gasped.

"I had a lot on my mind—that man on the train for a start," Bridget snapped. "For all I know, he might be dead, and I remember thinking that day that if they found him clutching my manicure case— oh, well, I don't suppose anything like that did happen. No news is good news, so they say."

"Oh, fine, fine!" groaned Felicity. "So you had it located and she's got it? Oh, golly, that means she might know who she is, then, now?"

She noticed for the first time that Bridget looked rather sick. "Yes, she does, and so does your brother. At least, they know a lot more about her, and it's all over the hospital. They say your brother looks terrible."

Felicity got to her feet. "Why?" she asked, through dry lips. "Why? What is it, then, that they found in that case?"

"It seems I didn't remember right," Bridget offered. "The luggage tab said *Mrs*. Lesley Weldon, and in the case there was a lot of trousseau things and . . . a wedding gown and orange blossom," she said, licking her lips. "I'm sorry, Felicity," and it was the first time Felicity had ever heard Bridget apologise.

7

FELICITY gaped. "I don't believe it!" she gasped. She stared at Bridget, willing her to say it was just another of her stupid jokes, but it was so obvious that Bridget was no longer joking. She was frankly frightened.

Felicity exclaimed, "My brother! I must go and find him!"

She couldn't get out of her mind's eye the way Maurice had looked at that girl. If he had fallen in love with her, what would he be feeling like now? She was terrified of facing him, yet she had to go and see him, with an unformed idea in her mind of asking him if it were really true, and if so, to let him know how sorry she was. Not that he would want any sympathy from her.

Alan West endorsed this idea, when he stopped Felicity in her headlong flight across to the hospital.

"Hey, where are you going to? Don't you know yet that you shouldn't run?"

He was the last person she had wanted to meet, and she shifted uncomfortably.

"I only wanted to see my brother. Something awful's happened. Bridget said—"

"I know," he said roughly. "Everyone knows. It's all over the hospital, and if you must know, I don't particularly want to hear what your friend Bridget said. Hasn't she caused enough trouble already?"

"But she didn't mean to," Felicity said confusedly.

"Look," he said, more gently, "I know how you feel, but take my word for it —your brother won't want to see you or anyone just now. Poor chap, I feel so sorry for him. For them both. I tried to say a few things and got my head bitten off for my pains, so I left him. As for her, I just don't know what's happened to her, but all I hope is that the shock might just jolt her memory back."

"Shouldn't you be trying to help her?" Felicity asked bluntly. "I mean, isn't it a job for a psychiatrist?"

He grinned lopsidedly at her. "That's what I said to your brother, but he didn't think so. He thought it was more in his field and invited me to keep out of it. We shall see. Here, let me walk you back to the Nurses' Home, and stop worrying. It isn't your fault, and anyway, if I've got the story right, it means that we're one step further forward in piecing together her background. It might just jolt her into remembering, but anyway, we've now got something to go on."

"What, for instance?" she asked glumly.

"We can now begin to search for a Mr. Weldon," he said quietly. "We know the chap's name, whereas before we didn't even know there was a husband around, did we?"

Into her frozen thoughts the reality thrust itself. Gone was Maurice's bright future with that girl, if all the signs had been read rightly and he had fallen in love with her. What would he do? How would he feel? She shuddered. It might be so terrible to find someone you could love, and then discover that they weren't even free!

"Felicity," Alan said gently, "you're off tomorrow too, aren't you? How would it be if I got the day off and took you a long way away so you wouldn't be tempted to approach your brother or get into more mischief with that impossible Bridget Moore?"

"All right," she said, without much enthusiasm. She was thinking of something else. What would the private enquiry agent engaged by Colonel Partridge do now? Would he just be paid off because he couldn't find the Thing but had found Bridget? Or would he stay on and discover who Lesley Weldon belonged to and how she came to be connected with Bridget on that train?

"Do I read you rightly, or don't you really care whether you come with me or not?" he asked bluntly. "I'm not sticking my neck out if you really hate the sight of me, you know!"

That jerked her back to him, as he had intended. Without thinking what she was saying, she blurted out: "If you want to know, I think I'd like nothing better than to be with you—I mean, you take things in hand and I don't have to worry—well, I mean, I *like*—"

"Yes?" he said softly. "You like . . . what were you going to say?"

She decided angrily that she really wanted her head searching. What could she have been thinking of, to almost admit that she liked the idea of being with him in what she termed glumly as her hour of need? She said instead, "Oh, I don't know what I was going to say, except that I liked the idea of having a sudden day out thrust upon me. Well, you must admit that things don't look so hot for me at the moment, especially as life is black for my brother Maurice!"

He had to be content with that. Felicity wasn't going to let herself blurt anything else out. She went back into the Home with his last-minute instructions for the next day ringing in her ears. "And don't keep me waiting!" he called last of all.

Alan then went to the nearest telephone

and called up Maurice to tell him he was taking Felicity out the next day. Maurice hesitated, but he couldn't grapple with this new problem. He wanted to ask Alan why he was so interested in a tiresome PTS girl, but he couldn't be bothered. He was too frozen with the shock of discovering that Lesley was married.

He thought if he lived to be a hundred he would never blot out of his mind her face as she lifted the lid of that case. Trousseau things—frothy lace and nylon, in a mad jumble, and lying on top, hastily flung in, a wedding gown of thick white lace, together with the veil and a silver circlet trimmed with clusters of orange blossom. She had looked frozen with fear, and her eyes, so dark, lifted to his in bewilderment.

Clearly she hadn't remembered any more than she had already, but those murkily veiled memories that tried to thrust themselves to the surface of her mind receded too hastily to be recognisable, and she had dropped the lid of the case and sat shuddering, her eyes fastened on the contents from where she sat, as if she expected something frightful to leap out at her.

Matron had gently taken everything out and held up each item for her to see, but nothing made sense to Lesley, and there was nothing in that case—no passport, for instance, or letters—to give any further clues.

Where was the bridegroom? he asked himself. He said to Lesley, "Is there nothing you can remember? Not even where you were going? What happened to your ticket?"

She had said, through stiff lips, "I expect *he* had them." He, the man with no face, no name, no identity, who had married her and presumably gone with her on that train, but left her . . . why? Or had she left him? Had she got off her own train and boarded another, in that dreadful lapse of memory? But if that were the case, surely, surely the man would be half crazy with anxiety, looking for her?

"I think it's a job for the police," he had said to Matron, and she had nodded

195

agreement and put out her hand for the telephone, when unexpectedly Lesley had gone to pieces. She must have heard that quiet remark of his.

"No! No police!" she sobbed, hanging on to his arm. "No, not the police, whatever happens! I don't know why. I only know you mustn't call in the police!"

In her present state, he felt he had to promise her that that shouldn't be done, and having made the promise and got her quiet and back into bed in a side ward this time, where she could have quiet and peace, he felt he couldn't go back on that promise.

Matron said, "I suppose it might be all right if we asked that enquiry agent of the Colonel's to do a little search and find? After all, we only promised her not to call in the police."

He had demurred, but Matron had said, "Well, the police would have questioned her first. We couldn't have stopped that and it would have been so distressing. But the enquiry agent would question other people instead. I do feel—" and he had

had to agree to the wisdom of that. So they had contacted the Colonel's man, who had after all located the slippery Bridget and the equally slippery Felicity in the crypt and heard their conversation, and given him what information they had.

"Will you want to question Bridget Moore?" Matron had asked, but he had smiled and shaken his head. "Hardly likely to be a productive source of information, I'm afraid," he had commented, and then went on to tell them that first he would check where the Weldons had been married and work from that angle.

Maurice, sick at heart, went back on duty. Work was the only cure for this. Work, and to somehow try to forget that a girl with serious dark eyes and a face that would have delighted the painter Rubens had twisted herself round his heart without any tricks or guile. A girl whose very helplessness and the gallant way she had tackled life without a memory had made him break a rule of a lifetime and get emotionally involved.

Well, if this didn't teach him, nothing

else would. And now he was going to have this extra burden to carry on his shoulders: his own crushing defeat the first time he had let himself love someone, as well as the burden of Felicity and the grandparents.

Finally he worked his way back to Sibylla Stansfield Ward. Mrs. Mobbs was very wretched. Her secret source of food supplies had been pounced on and stopped, and now, wretched and perpetually hungry, she was gradually losing weight. Hunger gnawed at her and made life miserable for her neighbours. And that night Mrs. Gadd haemorrhaged and had to be rushed up to theatre.

While Maurice had his work to keep him occupied and every nerve strained and every thought bent on saving a life and therefore unable to consider his own troubles, Lesley had nothing to keep her from thinking. She sat desperately in her own little room and wondered what was going to become of her.

It was a nice room, rather like a single room in a good hotel. She forced herself to consider it, and she was shocked to find that in this short while she had become attached to it. It was the only home she had now, and she was terrified of the thought of leaving it to go and meet some unknown man whose name was Weldon and whom she had apparently married. She stared at the mauve and green glazed print curtains and bed-cover, the pale green wash-basin and the white-painted furniture. The walls were a pale primrose shade, shining paintwork that reflected every scrap of sunshine. Unlike the other bedrooms, there were no personal things about—no photographs or pictures. But there was a clock that Maurice had lent her, because she would have overslept in the mornings without an alarm. There were a few books she had borrowed from the hospital library. A plastic brush and comb in pink, which clashed, because she hadn't been able to find a mauve or green set. Bottles of shampoo and the simplest set of make-up because there hadn't been much money in the small change purse of the unfamiliar plastic handbag, and she hadn't had any wages yet from her job in the hospital.

They were due on the following day, and to keep herself from thinking of the husband who was somewhere, and who apparently hadn't known how to go about finding her . . . or who perhaps didn't want to find her, a little voice persisted in her head.

She would go to a chain store the next day, she told herself firmly, and buy a picture frame, and cut out the picture on the cover of one of the magazines lying about in the sitting-room, and put it on the wall. Her own picture. She would buy a dressing-gown, a cheap and utilitarian one, because she couldn't bear the thought of using the trousseau dressing-gown in that case and she hadn't anything else. What other life had she been entering into, to need a dressing-gown of thick ring velvet, trimmed with a narrow band of fur? she asked herself blankly. What sort of husband had she had, who would offer her a life where she needed that sort of trousseau, and who hadn't been able to find her?

It was no use, she just couldn't keep her thoughts away from the subject. She lay down on the bed and tried to sleep, but the lights from the cars going by in the now darkened world outside made moving patterns across her ceiling, from right to left, and they mesmerised her. She just had to follow them, and they brought her to the train journey and she could almost hear the sound of the wheels on the lines, and the clashing sound they made going over the points. Sweat broke out all over her as she realised she was about to *remember*. On the edge of *knowing*.

She sat up, shaking all over, and the elusive memory slid back again into oblivion. She was glad. She would have pushed it back herself, if she could have. It was then that she realised what Maurice had meant, about the mind not wanting to remember. She didn't want her mind to work, because there was something, something there in the background that was completely unacceptable.

She couldn't stay there alone. She felt she would go mad. The pretty walls seemed as if they were pressing in on her. She jumped up off the bed and slipped into her jacket and went out.

Bridget saw her go, and went back into Felicity's room to tell her, but the telephone started to ring. It was a call for her from Eileen Shelley. Felicity came out, her eyebrows raised in enquiry, just like the old days. They had always told each other about telephone calls. From a lifelong habit, Bridget covered the receiver and said briefly, "Eileen Shelley—you know, photo studio," and returned to take her call.

Eileen was upset. "Bridget, you little wretch, do you realise the mess you've got us all into?"

"It seems to me," Bridget said smartly, "that people seem to think it's a good plan to blame everything on to me. How on earth can I make a mess for you, if I'm stuck here in the hospital—you won't believe this, but I'm training to be a nurse."

"I don't care if you're training to be a nut who goes up to the moon, you've indirectly made a mess for us all, but it was you who made it. Do you *know* what that guardian of yours is doing?"

Bridget wearily said she didn't and that she couldn't care less.

"Then you'd better care," said Eileen, in a tone that was very angry indeed. "He's making enquiries about some valuable thing that was missing when you went, and he seems to think that poor old Frank had something to do with it. He's sending a detective person poking around all our places, and it's sending Felix up the wall because the poor old boy has some activities—well, let's face it, one doesn't always want people to know how one makes a living, although it might not necessarily be on the outside of the law. And it's all your fault, you little wretch!"

"Oh, no, it isn't." Bridget was now angry herself. "If Frank had an absolutely clear conscience he wouldn't need to worry about that clot of a detective my guardian is using. My friend Felicity led him an awful dance all over the place when he was following her and he only found us by accident and an awful slice of good luck."

"And your guardian," Eileen Shelley continued, as if she hadn't even listened to what Bridget was saying, "is of the opinion that you took it to Frank and he gave you something for it because you were short of cash and that Frank found a buyer and made a packet out of it. Just because Frank is an art dealer and has customers who might just know what the thing is and what it is worth. It just isn't fair!"

"Quite apart from my having already told everyone (and that includes my guardian) that I had the thing on me by mistake and lost it in the upholstery in the railway carriage," Bridget said sarcastically, "just what is your interest in Frank all of a sudden? As I remember it, you two were always at each other in the past and you never had a good word for him."

"I don't know what you're talking about," Eileen said in a peculiar tone. "Frank and I have always been good friends, being in the same sort of trade— well, he sells pictures and—"

"—you take them," Bridget finished, confident she had made a huge pun and starting to laugh in that queer, infectious whooping way of hers.

Felicity came to the door again. "Shut up, you ass! Look, everyone's coming to their doors! You may not know it, but some people are doing homework for their exams."

"More fool them," Bridget said succinctly, and to round off the conversation, she went on: "All right, I get the message. You are now soppy over Frank and you're kidding yourself he's going to ask you to marry him. Well, I wish you joy of each other—"

Eileen's conversation came through to Bridget, overriding her own words. "—and what you don't seem to realise is that I'm giving you a hint as to the way the wind is blowing. There's some fellow called Claude Langley, he's a sort of confidence trickster, I suppose. Someone saw you with him on the train. And there's some talk about a girl who was with you —a dark girl, with dark eyes and hair, and she was wearing a brown suit—"

Bridget went very still. "Would you say that all over again, Eileen? Well, all right, I got the description, but what about her?"

"You were seen carrying her case, after you'd both split up. Your guardian's detective got that much by way of his first round of snooping. Don't ask how I found out. Let's just say I have a very marked degree of hearing—"

"Well, what were you doing near enough to a keyhole that would let you listen in to my guardian and his detective talking?" Bridget retorted, but her thoughts were racing. "Anyway, you got it all wrong. I explained all that to him. To both of them. I don't know the girl. I just saw her sitting by me on the train—"

"—and she's at your hospital and there's a very funny story been given by way of explanation. Your guardian isn't going to be taken in by that oldie story about amnesia, you know. It's been done to death."

"But it's true!" Bridget squeaked.

Eileen ignored that. "And if you want another hint for free, from an old friend, it's this: don't underestimate your guardian's private eye. That rather naïve look of his is his particular stock-in-trade. He does very well on it, but he's nobody's fool," and without listening for what Bridget had to comment on that, Eileen said a curt goodbye and rang off.

Felicity said, "I've explained to them all that you were taken by surprise and that you won't make any more row and they've all gone back into their rooms, but you'd better be quiet. Come in and tell me what all that was about."

Bridget went in and glumly sat on Felicity's bed. The other two girls were in Linda Howland's room, because even if she hadn't the brains to help them with their work, she was at least quiet, which was more than could be said for Felicity and Bridget, who chattered all the time. Bridget said now, "Are you sure that that girl with no memory is really above board? I mean, you wouldn't think she'd pinched the Thing from me, and is madly pretending she can't recall a thing?"

Felicity was shocked and said so.

"What a rotten thing to say! I like her and I'm sure that isn't the case! Besides, she's had something awful happen to her. Maurice says so. And she had that case full of trousseau things—"

"But it might not be hers," urged Bridget. "That name might not be hers. She might have pinched the case from someone. She hasn't got a wedding ring nor an engagement ring, and there isn't a mark on her hand to show she ever had one. Everyone says so. If you want my honest opinion, it's all jolly peculiar."

"My brother Maurice says—"

"Don't boil over to me," Bridget said quickly. "Your brother Maurice is soppy over her, so he'd say anything. But I'm beginning to ask myself a few questions about her."

"Just because Eileen Shelley has been talking," Felicity jeered. "Not so long back, you couldn't stand her. Not so long back, I telephoned her to find out where you were in case something had happened to you—"

"What, for heaven's sake?"

"You could have been kidnapped or run over and a casualty in some other hospital or anything might have happened to you. But did she care? Not her! All she could think of was taking a beastly shot of some bawling child in her studio and she just demanded that we got off the line and bothered someone else to help us find someone called Bridget Moore."

"What does that prove?"

"That she doesn't care about you, but you're prepared to believe anything she says about that nice girl who happens to have amnesia, just because you've got a suspicious mind and not a shred of kindness in you."

They glared at each other. Felicity had done it again. She had let her tongue run away with her and said what she wouldn't admit to herself. That Bridget was no good.

Bridget stood her ground. "I don't like that girl and I'm going out of my way to prove that she's got the Thing, and I'm going to set the guardian's private eye on her, because she's a menace, and that's what! She must be a menace, because she works all decent men round her little finger. Even the porters won't have a word said about her, and they're a lot of tough nuts, if there ever were any! She's even got Matron silly over her, and I heard some of the second-years saying you couldn't fool Matron! They don't know what that Lesley Weldon is really like!"

"You're just sour because you're not holding the centre of the stage any more," Felicity retorted, but she wasn't far from the truth, though she didn't know it.

"Anyway," Bridget said, having the last word, "she happens to have gone out, at this time of night, and you can't tell me she's up to any good, to do that."

"What's wrong with going out for a breath of air, if you don't go too far?" Felicity flashed back.

"How do we know she hasn't gone far, and if she really *has* amnesia, do you think she'd risk going out on her own at night?

I wouldn't and I bet you wouldn't, nor anyone else. Which just proves that she hasn't lost her memory any more than you or me, and I'm going to tell someone."

"You just do, that's all," snapped Felicity, "and I will personally have great pleasure in telling everyone a few things about you that so far have been kept personal and private."

Bridget hesitated, and decided it wasn't worth the effort of betraying Lesley's movements. But it was a wasted effort, because one of the porters saw Lesley go out and he was sufficiently worried about her to search around to find the RMO.

Maurice was just leaving a patient. Mrs. Gadd was down from theatre. He had seen the latest admission and there was nothing else he could do for her. He went down with drooping shoulders and stood outside, sniffing the good clean air and looking up at the hard brilliance of the stars, when the porter approached him.

"Perhaps I'm worrying unnecessarily, sir," he began, "but that new young lady with the lost memory has gone out alone—"

Maurice jumped. "Alone?"

"That's right, sir. She had a sort of funny look on her face, sort of blank, somehow, or else I would have shouted after her. I didn't quite know what to do, so I thought I'd hunt around to find you and tell you."

"Which way did she go?" Maurice demanded, tearing off his white coat which he had forgotten to remove before he left the hospital.

The porter told him. Maurice started to go on foot, but decided it would be quicker to take his car. She might be too tired herself to walk back, if she had been wandering far.

He drove slowly along the streets of Uxley Green, combing the people on the pavements and crossing the roads, searching among the traffic as he drove, and thinking all the time of the things amnesia patients did and wondering what would become of Lesley, himself, all the people connected with him, and moreover, what had become of that husband of hers: the mysterious Mr. Weldon who was so profligate where that beautiful creature's safety and well-being was concerned.

He was almost on the point of giving up, when he saw her, leaning on the parapet of the bridge, staring down at the river. He drove on, searching for and finding a place to leave his car, with rare good luck on this occasion, and then running back, praying she would still be there. He dared not admit what he had been thinking, fearing . . . but she was still there.

She turned at the sound of his footsteps and a glad smile broke over her face as she recognised him. That smile destroyed all his resolutions not to touch her, and he took her into his arms without quite realising what he was doing. She didn't help, by going straight to him as if she belonged to him. They clung briefly, desperately, then he put her from him. "Come on, my dear, let's get back to the hospital. You shouldn't be out alone at night. Uxley Green isn't quite the place—"

"Not yet, Maurice. Don't let's go back yet," she pleaded. "Let's walk down there for a bit. It looks so quiet and peaceful. I was gathering up courage to go down by myself, but . . ."

"I'm glad you didn't!" he said at once. "Promise me you wouldn't do such a thing, ever!" And she promised. Readily, as if she'd promise anything he asked, because she was so glad he was there with her.

They went down the steps by the bridge. It was broad here, and safe, but he wouldn't take her along the narrow path that wound its way to the lock. Too many casualties came from that quarter. He wasn't going to add to her already clouded, tragic young life, by running into trouble. He could hear a band of youths singing, up on the bridge.

But they went, and it was quiet again, and she said, her voice clear and warm in the stillness, "I couldn't stay alone in my room any more. I kept thinking of that man I'm supposed to be married to, and that one day he'll come for me and I shall have to go away with him, and he'll be a stranger and I won't want to go. Maurice, I don't want to be with anyone else but you. What am I going to do?"

"When he comes," Maurice forced himself to say, "you may well remember everything, and be glad to see him, and I shall just be the doctor who tried to help you when you couldn't remember anything."

"No. *No*! No, Maurice, I don't *feel*, inside me, that I'm married. I don't feel that anything nice had happened in my life. It's just someone I fear, or something —it makes me feel so awful that I have to stop being alone and get among other people and then it isn't so bad. If he comes back, Maurice, I shall run away."

"Promise me you won't do any such thing," he said urgently. "You must not! Be fair—you don't know that he's the one who is frightening you."

"I believe that if all was as it should be, I couldn't have lost my memory," she said firmly. "I was sitting alone in my room— actually lying down, trying to sleep—and

I was on the train again, and I could hear the sound of the train, and I could almost smell the special train smell, and I think he was on that train, because I could feel the memory coming back, and it was so awful, I couldn't bear to let it come, so I jumped up and came straight out, and I wouldn't let myself think."

"Oh, my dear," he groaned, and she leaned against him and reached up and put her cheek against his, and his arm slid round her, protectively, no passion in the gesture now. He felt so helpless, wanting to protect her, not knowing what to do for the best.

"Maurice, your sister said there was no one in your life. Is that really true? Don't just shake your head—tell me. Say so! What about that staff nurse?"

He took her face in his hands and looked into her eyes. They were so dark in the pallor of her face, and there was, in the moonlight, a breathtaking yet ethereal beauty about her that sometimes frightened him. He felt that she might slip through his fingers and the loss would be too great to bear, and it was always worse at night. She lost that frail look in the daytime.

"My dearest, if I were to say there was no one, it wouldn't be true, yet I haven't the right to. If you want the truth, it's you . . . only you, filling my life so that I can't think of anything else, can't do anything without you're there crowding out all coherent thought. It's like sickening for a bug. I'm sorry to put it like that, but there it is, because d'you see, you belong to someone else (we know that!), yet I can't stop loving you. I love you, Lesley, only you! There never has been anyone else! I didn't want to say it, but I have, and much good may it do either of us."

"It will do me good," she said contentedly, cuddling against him. "I'm glad, so glad you feel like that, because I feel like that about you. I don't care if I've ever been in love before. I don't care who's in my life, that I've forgotten. It can't have been like this. It just can't have been like this!"

He didn't answer. He had seen too many

amnesia patients before, and he knew well the cold look of surprise and dislike in their faces for the people who had been so close to them and helped them while the state of amnesia had lasted.

8

FOR Felicity, all this lost its importance. Her PTS exam came up. The rest of the batch who had started the same day as she had were looking anxious and a little scared. With the exception of Linda Howland, who was, after all, much more interested in the physical training side than pure nursing, and no doubt had a future there alone, the others needed to pass this exam so badly. Felicity said nothing, but glumly trailed in with the rest of them.

Lesley, out to tea with Maurice that day, said, with a small smile, "Do you think your young sister will pass her exam?"

He didn't want to talk about Felicity. He just wanted to sit and look at Lesley. She was wearing a new dress; a cool white dress with stripes of fawn and black, with starchy white cuffs and collar. Everyone else that day in Uxley Green was following slavishly the current fashion, but Lesley had found a dress that had, he remembered from the days at home, been called a shirt-waister. With its full skirt and formal top, it made her look so different from every other woman, and so *right*, somehow. His heart ached when he permitted his thoughts to wander to the subject of what her future would be, and it was in a rather vague tone that he said, "She might. She might just have a slice of luck and squeeze through. I wouldn't put it past her."

She watched the people go by as she asked softly, "Is it a difficult exam? What do they have to do?"

He thought she was just making conversation, so that she, too, wouldn't have to think ahead, so he pandered to her, and told her all about it.

"It's difficult if you've been tiresome and not worked as you should, or if you haven't the gift of keeping in your head the names of the instruments and diseases or being able to spell them. You need a certain amount of good—well, explicit, anyway—English."

This brought a smile to her lips. "English. That used to be my weak subject."

He went suddenly very still, watching her. She looked quickly at him. "What made me say that? How do I know what it was like? And yet I know it to be true. Am I going to remember, Maurice?"

It was such a scared whisper. He said, "Yes, if you let it ride, come back when it will. Think of something else—my sister Felicity and her chances today. She'll never pass the bed-making test, for a start. Five kinds of bed—operation, heart, rheumatism, fracture, etc—and she can't make a normal bed! How to administer oxygen will be, I imagine, a beautiful mystery to her, and if she has to give an injection or a blanket bath, my poor sister will do something so original that the whole examining body will collapse, not just Sister Tutor! And that's only the practical side. So far as I know," he went on thoughtfully, "she doesn't even know

221

there are such things as trolleys to be laid up. And then we have the little problem of the written papers. I wonder what made our grandparents think she might manage to become a nurse?"

"Your grandparents. Tell me about them," Lesley begged.

He smiled. They were dear to his heart and he loved her for wanting to know about them.

"They are very modern and until quite recently, very active. Not, however, active enough to cope with Felicity, but then there are times when even I don't feel active enough for that!"

That made her smile brilliantly, and his expression altered as he watched her. She turned away in embarrassment.

"My grandparents," he continued, "are very tall people, with white hair. My grandmother uses make-up and spends a lot of time and money at the hairdressers. She attends a lot of committee meetings, and takes a big hand in the social life of the church and parish. That sort of people," he finished, not even sure if she was listening.

She was watching a man, a tall, rangy man of anything between thirty-five and forty. A very shrewd type of man, forceful and confident. He was watching the traffic, waiting to catch an empty cruising taxi. He carried a briefcase.

"What is it?" Maurice asked sharply.

"I feel . . . I know him," she faltered. "At least, that I've seen him before."

"Take it easy," he said gently. "Just let things ride," and all the time he was hoping against hope that that wasn't the man who was her husband. A man who was too smart by half, a confidence trickster, was the thought that came into Maurice's mind.

The man found his cab and got in. He leaned across and murmured, "St. Mary's Hospital," and sat back. The cab took a long time to get through the traffic, but when they reached the high red brick wall round the Nurses' Home, the tall man tapped on the glass and told the driver to stop there. That, he said, would do.

After he had paid off the taxi, he strolled all round the hospital. It was quite a long walk and took him some time, but he wasn't in any hurry. He noticed the lilac overalls and caps of the PTS girls, the entirely different uniform of the student nurses. He regarded, and quickly discarded, the scarlet belts of the SRNs and the unusual grey of the Ward Sisters' uniforms. He knew enough about hospitals to know that the PTS girls were the smallest fry, the lowest form of animal life in the hospital, so he didn't make the mistake of asking for the one he wanted. It shouldn't be difficult. Quite apart from looking for that tantalisingly ugly lilac uniform, he also had to look for red hair. The combination, he thought with some distaste, should be quite revolting.

Bridget, whom he sought, passed close by him, but her hair was so brassily blonde, it fooled him. He looked right past her and strolled on.

Bridget was thoroughly alarmed. This was Claude Langley, the man she had met on the train; the man who had thought he could get the Thing from her by the very unsubtle means of a little cuddle and tickle in the luggage van. Her lip curled in disdain as she recalled his tactics. He must have got himself out of the dell where he jumped from the train, and it must have taken him some time to get rid of his bruises. Perhaps he had by now had a chance to examine the package and find it was only her flat manicure case. He would be pretty wild, she considered. She had no illusions as to his type. Bridget, at eighteen and a bit, had had a quite remarkable experience of men, and had met all sorts. This type was fun to be with for the odd half an hour, in the apparent safety of a long-distance train, but not to have coming round the hospital, making a nuisance of himself.

She watched him from the cover of the wall jutting out from the path. lab. He was looking for her and he wasn't going to go from there until he had found her. She decided she must do something about it. She had, like a ninny, told him where she was bound for, how much she loathed the idea of becoming a nurse, and of how awful she would look, with her red hair, in that lilac uniform. She hadn't expected to see him again, so it hadn't seemed to matter. One pair of ears to listen to her woes was very much like another.

But now he was here, and he would no doubt make things very difficult for her if she couldn't think of some way in which to get rid of him.

She was bored and restless. The others were doing their exam., and from what Felicity had told her about the part already done, she was pretty sure that she herself could have got through most of it, even though she had only been there a few weeks.

With time on her hands and that man outside, she had to get things moving. She just couldn't keep standing, staring from behind curtains, walls, waiting for him to go. She made up her mind to test out whether he remembered her face, so she changed out of the lilac uniform and put on a summer dress and sun-glasses, then walked past him, close to him.

She had almost got by when he spoke to her. "I'm looking for a student with red hair, called Bridget Moore," he began pleasantly.

Bridget had almost dropped in her tracks when he had stopped her. She was sure he remembered her. Well, he would do when he heard her voice, so instead of answering, she shrugged, giggled, vaguely pointed and walked on.

She half turned to cross the road and found he hadn't moved but was standing there staring, perplexed. He probably recognised her walk, too!

She must do something about it, she told herself. As always, she had the urge to change the colour of her hair, and with the money she had got from pawning the very good watch she had been wearing, she also bought a new dress and changed it in the shop. But she couldn't do much about her face. Even with a new hair-cut (this time a close boyish cut with a thick fringe) and the pale brown shade that was very much like the one she had been bequeathed by nature, Bridget felt she hadn't changed very much. She still had what she termed a 'definite' kind of walk, but which Felicity would have called, in her most unfriendly mood towards Bridget, a frankly inviting walk with a come-hither wiggle at the hips.

She paused to examine her new self in the mirror at the back of a leather goods window, and saw in passing a new leather briefcase very much like the brash new one that Claude Langley had been carrying. Without pausing to think Bridget plunged into the shop and bought it, and sharply invited the shop people to leave the crumpled paper packing inside it, so that it looked filled with papers.

She hadn't any formed idea of what she was going to do with it, but the old trick of switching briefcases of gentlemen on the Board of Governors at her old school was always good for making the masculine mind get the message that it wasn't welcome. Without having it wrapped, she walked smartly back to the hospital. Briefcase and package containing the dress she had gone out wearing, and the brown short hair and sun-glasses, did fool Claude Langley, who was still standing there. There wasn't much of the briefcase visible, behind the other package and a bag of cherries she had stopped to buy from a stall at the end of the road, and in Claude's opinion, any girl who staggered along laden like that, and with that unattractive shade of hair and very little make-up, didn't really qualify for a second glance.

Felicity, tired out after the exams, was lying flat on her back on her bed. She dragged herself up into a sitting position, saying, "Good heavens, what on earth have you done to yourself? I didn't recognise you!"

"Good! It's too much to hope that wretch at the gates won't recognise me, although I've just walked past him. I simply must get rid of him and make him not want to come again," and she told Felicity what the significance was. "Got any ideas?"

"Oh, no, you don't," Felicity said quickly. "I almost started to think up a few, but not any more! Not for me! I

229

might have gone into mad pranks with you at school, but if I have managed to scrape through that exam. today, I want to go on to the wards, and that lets me out of bright ideas to work off on your men-friends, Bridget!"

"Meanie," Bridget said without rancour. "Then I'll have to ask that fat girl down the corridor. She's too stupid to see any risk in it. Look, all I want is to invite him in to wait in the sitting-room, and then, when he's put down his briefcase, I want a shindy started outside, so he comes out, without briefcase, to lend a strong masculine hand."

Felicity stared, then shook her head. "No can do! Faulty reasoning, anyway. He wouldn't let his briefcase out of his hand, if it contained anything valuable. What do you think it would contain?"

"I don't know," Bridget said blankly. "Sandwiches, I shouldn't wonder. Oh, and probably business papers. I couldn't care less."

"Then why cause me to risk my future at this hospital just to—"

"I'd be doing you a service getting you out of here before you become all puffed up with the thought of the future dedicated nurse you aim to be carrying off gold medals and effecting rescues on the roof and earning a trip to the Palace to be decorated and all that. I'm the best friend you ever had!"

"I doubt that," Felicity said dryly. "Listen, just why do you suppose he came here? To look for you?"

"Well, he asked for me, didn't he? I bet he's discovered I dished him over the Thing. At the best, he still wants to persuade me to sell it to him for little or nothing, and at the worst he wants to skin me for making such a fool of him, wrapping up a manicure set and passing it off for a treasure."

"Well, if he wants something that badly, he won't be fobbed off by someone pinching his briefcase," Felicity said sensibly.

"You're scared, that's what. Or else gone goody-goody with the idea of becoming a nice pudding-faced nursie.

Yah! How I despise people who get filled with the desire to do a dull good honest day's work. Okay, leave me to do the job myself, or better still, ask the fat girl."

Felicity dragged herself off her bed. "I don't suppose I've passed my exams., and come to think of it, it might be less ordinary to be kicked out for a scrape than to be just sent home as incompetent. That way they'd know I had no brains, but the other way there'd always be a doubt. Right, come on! What's the big idea?"

Bridget grinned hugely and threw a heavy arm round Felicity's shoulder. "Atta-girl! Just like the old days," and down the stairs they went together. "Now this is the idea, with room for improvement, of course. I go out and do my cleft palate stuff, like in that awful play at school, remember—"

"No, because no one understood you!" Felicity protested.

"Well, the lisp, then. And I'll give him to understand that if he comes in to wait, Bridget will appear. Then, once he's in the sitting-room, we'll pull the cupboard over and scream blue murder for help—"

"—and fetch Home Sister, to say nothing of everyone in the building!" Felicity said scathingly, dismissing the idea.

"All to the good!" Bridget said, thinking. "The way I see it is, it's brilliant! We want to create a diversion to get him out of that nice lonely private little room, don't we? Away from that briefcase so I can switch it."

"While I'm heaving a cupboard over?" Felicity exploded. "Don't be funny! That cupboard's heavy—it's full of books and papers!"

"Perfect!" said Bridget. "Nothing to break—just a lot of old books and stuff, and you wouldn't have to heave it yourself —I'd help you. And it isn't all that heavy, I bet! Then, while you're screaming for help, having realistically (and noisily) fallen down in the process—"

"Thank you very much! I shall be bruised all over!"

"—I will nip round to the french windows—"

"—which will be bolted inside, you dope."

"I shall have first seen to it that they were unbolted," Bridget said loftily.

Felicity was wavering. She hadn't left Bridget at school so long ago; the days of their great and well-thought-out scrapes weren't so far in the distant past, and the voice that had tempted her then could still tempt her. She sighed, "Oh, well, it can't do any harm, I suppose. That cupboard isn't very steady—I heard one of the maids say so only the other day." She bit her lip. "If only I could be convinced that it would do some good, though. I don't see what you hope to achieve. You know, Bridget, it wouldn't be the first time that you told me one story as a reason, and then I afterwards found that the ulterior motive was quite different and one that would have prevented me from agreeing anyway."

Bridget looked offended. "You don't have to agree! Come to think of it, you've made it pretty clear since I've been here that you've gone off me, so why don't you leave it to the fat girl? I think she'd be a pretty good stooge (I mean, partner) and at least she wouldn't keep showing how chicken she was, which is what you are!"

Felicity's face flamed. Her caution in the past had always been branded as cowardice by Bridget when Bridget had wanted to score a point, and it was the same now.

Bridget, quietly triumphant, led the way downstairs to the cupboard in the hall, Felicity, hot and indignant, following her.

To her life's end, Felicity told herself afterwards, she would never cease to wonder why that cry of 'chicken' produced the required results so often. Why hadn't she *let* Bridget sneer at her for being a coward? But that was afterwards, a long time afterwards. Meantime the old love of adventure and fun chased away from Felicity her newly acquired virtuous desire to become a sedate student nurse. Bridget went out and fetched the man in, and told him primly that she would tell Home Sister he was there and fetch Bridget

Moore for him. Her lisp sickened Felicity, who felt sure that that man, who looked as hard-boiled and world-weary as any she had seen, must surely be aware that he was being shepherded into that room to wait, by Bridget Moore herself.

Then Felicity had a bad moment. Bridget came out and she said urgently to her, "The french windows! You didn't go and unbolt them!"

Bridget looked a bit pale, she thought, but their luck appeared to be in. "I know. I thought of that when I was in there, but I looked. The doors are unbolted anyway. So it's all right."

Claude Langley prowled around the room. He hated small rooms, but he was aware that after all that waiting, he would never get to see Bridget if he didn't do it the orthodox way like this. He put his briefcase down to go over to the book-shelves and examine some rather unusual specimens brought home from someone's foreign travels. Home Sister believed in sharing her treasures with everyone. They were all about all over the Home.

He was so engrossed in examining the bottom of a piece of porcelain that he didn't, for the moment, realise the significance of the scuffling outside, until he heard the crash. It didn't need Felicity's scream for help to make him do the obvious thing and open the door and run out. At that time there weren't too many people near that end of the Nurses' Home, and he found himself, with Home Sister and a couple of young nurses, with the brunt of the work of lifting a heavy cupboard and piles of books and papers off one girl's ankle.

Bridget thought confusedly, as she ran round to the french windows, that Felicity was a jolly good actress. That scream really sounded as if someone were in pain. She must remember to tell her not to overdo it next time.

Meantime she had to concentrate on switching the briefcase, then she realised she hadn't got the other one there. She had left it on the table in the hall by the cupboard. Oh, well, someone would find it for him and he would think he had carried it out there, she supposed, as she ran off with his.

But it wasn't shut. As she ran, it burst open and everything fell out. Panic-stricken now, she bundled everything up off the grass; her own manicure case, in its opened wrappings—evidently the reason he had come to see her—a lot of private papers, and a newspaper with an incredibly old date on it. Well, at least a month ago. She decided to have a look at that in her room. People didn't keep old newspapers and carry them about in a carefully guarded briefcase for nothing.

She went up another (and forbidden) staircase to their shared room, and sat down on her bed with the contents of the case spread about her. As she looked, her eyes opened wider, and her heart began to bump faster. She had plenty of nerve, but it now dawned on her that she wasn't playing around with a callow young man like Toby Fairbairn or any of the others she had met and who had eaten out of her hand. This was a man with a purpose, and he wasn't going to take kindly to any nonsense from a couple of student nurses, not considering what he had in mind. Even at a glance, she didn't need to be told that the things in this briefcase pertained to the private affairs of several people, all unknown to each other, and that he was following up these affairs for a purpose she didn't care about. No wonder he had been so smart over recognising possibilities in the possession of the Thing that had belonged to her guardian! This man knew what he was about.

She flicked through the newspaper, but there wasn't time to read it when she had found what it probably was being kept for. Regretfully, listening to the footsteps coming along the corridor, she realised the other two girls were returning. She bundled the things into the briefcase and thrust it under her bed, just in time before Ann Taylor and Kathy Milburn came in.

"Hello, hello, what have we got here? Successful candidates for ward duty?" she quipped, while she strove to regain her usual confident air.

The other two stared at each other,

exchanged an uneasy glance, then said, "Have you been in this room all the afternoon, then?"

"Why?" she asked warily.

"Well, you must have been," they told each other. "Or else you couldn't not have known, having had to come through the main hall."

Her heart missed a beat, then she realised that they wanted to tell her about the overturned cupboard and the mess everywhere. So she said, "Well, I heard a bit of a bang, but it didn't seem worth investigating. Go on, you both want to tell me all about it. What was it?"

They exchanged another of those irritating glances, then Kathy decided to be the one to tell her. "It was awful! Poor Mann! It *would* have to be her! I don't *know* what the RMO will say!"

Bridget felt uneasy. "What about Mann? And what's it got to do with the RMO, anyway?"

"A cupboard fell over on top of her, and her brother is out. Dr. Morris had to see to her."

"See to her?" Bridget squeaked, and then the awful truth began to dawn on her. Felicity hadn't been overacting, after all. She must have been really hurt!

9

FELICITY'S accident affected so many people in so many different ways. Lying there in acute pain in the high bed with the cage over one leg, she watched the succession of people coming and going.

Now she was at the receiving end. Now she knew what it would be like to be a patient, and in some queer way she knew that this experience had cut her off from Bridget for ever. It marked a gulf between them. Felicity couldn't have found the words to express what she felt exactly, but the actual living through the terror of that accident, lying there pinned under the cupboard, and afterwards being whipped off to be X-rayed, and up to theatre to have her leg set—all these things she now knew about and Bridget didn't. Bridget would go on blundering through with her inability to see the other person's point of view. Felicity herself would be able to nurse and *know* what it was like.

She saw her brother's face through new eyes. She hated herself for being the cause of that weariness and deep anxiety, that terrible distress, when he bent over her bed and touched her cheek. He had never shown such tenderness for her before, and he didn't say anything: as if his throat were frozen and he couldn't speak at all.

That girl—the one with the amnesia—came with him, and she stood and stared down at Felicity with a very odd look on her face. She didn't speak either; she just grasped Felicity's nearest hand and held it for a few minutes, then with the smallest smile she turned and went, with Maurice. The way those two walked off together struck Felicity as if they were already moulding their lives into one, fusing their personalities. They blended, she thought in amazement.

People coming with gifts, tiptoeing in and out if she appeared to be sleeping: no sojourn in the sick bay of the Nurses' Home but a private room off the surgical

243

wards, with the surgeons really concerned over her at one time. And Maurice coming and going like an uneasy ghost. But the one person she wanted to visit her didn't come.

She asked Maurice about him one day. "Where is your pal the psychiatrist?" It had to be kept light, so that he didn't get ideas.

Maurice said, "What do you want to know about Alan West for? Missing his scolding you?"

"Well, it came regular and often, and it is a thing to miss," she retorted, with a flash of the old spirit. "I suppose he's still around—or have they kicked him out?"

Maurice looked surprised. "No, they haven't kicked him out. They're not likely to. What's more to the point, we're afraid we shall lose him to London where his services will be better paid."

So that was it, Felicity told herself. He was going. On the point of leaving for a better berth, and hadn't got the decency to come and see her before he went. All right-y, she told herself furiously, keeping her eyes shut tightly so that Maurice shouldn't read in them her acute disappointment. All right-y, so if that's the way it's going to be, who cares? And she made up her mind to forget all about him and give her attention to the other men in her life.

There were plenty. All the young men in the hospital who had taken her dancing at the socials and playing tennis—the people she had known from the start of those hectic twelve weeks in PTS. Gifts and flowers from them and interesting little offerings from an unknown admirer, who might be anyone from Maurice's own friends down to the doting porters, who had good-naturedly cursed her mischief when she was around and who were now heartbroken to think what had happened to her.

No one would say just what the injury was, and it was sickening. The girls who had shared her room—Ann and Kathy and Linda—all looked acutely nervous when she asked them on their frequent visits.

"We don't know," they chorused. "No

one tells us anything," then went on to tell her about the results of the exam.

"You know you passed, of course?" That was the biggest surprise of anything, and not in any way dampened by their adding, all in one voice: "You only scraped through, but you did it!" She had done it, and what did it matter if she had only just scraped through? She could now go on the wards! That, to Felicity, was bliss.

If only Alan had come to see her, and if only they had allowed Bridget to come, just the once, so that they could talk over what had led to this accident and get things clarified: all would have been reasonably well again.

Alan didn't come, but Bridget was allowed, because Felicity got quite worked up about their refusing Bridget permission to visit.

Bridget had a hunted expression which was new to her.

"I say, how are you?" she began. "I didn't mean to do this—I can't see how I was responsible even now, and of course no one else knows. Unless you've told them?"

"What are you talking about?" Felicity demanded.

"Well, it was my idea about messing about with that cupboard, and I should have stopped to see if you were clear at your end, I suppose!"

"Listen, you dope," Felicity said earnestly, "it was my fault. I skidded on a bit of over-polished floor and went under the thing again as it was falling. You weren't to blame for that. I should have had more sense!"

"Yes, I was to blame, for persuading you to go into the thing with me. The worst of it is, it hasn't done the trick—keeping him away, I mean."

Felicity was wary now. Bridget looked anxiously at her. Felicity's new spent voice wasn't lost on Bridget, and she had been warned not to upset Felicity.

"He still haunts the place," Bridget went on.

Felicity paled. "You'll have to tell someone!"

"How can I? Can you imagine what it would be like? 'Please, Home Sister, I talked Mann into overturning the cupboard—so I was really the cause of bashing her ankle—to create a diversion so that the man, who I have reason to think is a confidence trickster, that I met and flirted with on the train, and now waiting in your waiting-room, should come out while I switched his briefcase for another so I could examine the contents, and now he's livid and is haunting the place and I'm afraid he'll do me a mischief so I don't go out'. Oh, fine, fine! Can't you see Home Sister's bulgy eyes coming out on stalks? (I say, I can't stand that woman, can you?) And how do you suppose it would be when they asked me if I was in the habit of scraping acquaintances for fun on trains and I had to admit that anything was in my line, so long as there was fun attached to it!"

"We were a couple of oafs, when you put it like that," Felicity said in a small voice.

"We've done it before," Bridget

reminded her. "The trouble is, this chap doesn't take no for an answer. He means to tear the place apart to get hold of the Thing, you know! Oh, and the contents of the briefcase—I didn't get a chance to tell you, did I? They were the oddest things! All private details that the people wouldn't want known."

"What sort of details?" Felicity whispered.

"Well, you know—old newspaper accounts of someone who ran away with someone else's husband, and a solicitor who was kicked out of his firm on suspicion of funny business, although they couldn't prove anything, things like that. Sounds like blackmail to me, though he wouldn't carry them about with him, would he? Not unless he'd just found those old newspapers after combing through the old files somewhere and nicking them when people weren't looking."

"Your language doesn't improve," Felicity remarked.

"It doesn't when things are exciting," Bridget said carelessly. "And here's another thing—in an old newspaper about a month old, there was a bit about your brother Maurice's girl-friend who's supposed to have lost her memory. Amnesia, my eye! That's a good one. I daresay she'll be having a visit from Claude Langley if he finds she's in this hospital."

Felicity looked thoroughly alarmed now. Bridget got up. "Hey, take it easy! I wouldn't have told you if I'd thought— Here, I'm going!"

Felicity tried to sit up, and screamed out with pain. Bridget ran for it, and just escaped the nurse who came at the double. She called Sister, who said, "That does it! I thought I wasn't doing the right thing, letting that girl come and visit you, Miss Mann, and what the RMO would say, I can't imagine!"

Bridget really held the centre of the stage after that episode. Colonel Partridge came. He was furious because his private eye had had no luck so far. He was still combing through registers and church entries to find the marriage. It was surprising how many couples named Weldon had got married in the last month or so, and they all had to be contacted and interviewed. The Colonel had lost his American buyer, who reasonably thought there was funny business. There was no insurance and the Colonel didn't like losing a lot of money like that, especially when it was the fault of his tiresome ward.

Matron was very angry that all these things should have been going on under her nose, and Sister Tutor and Home Sister were also very much put out. There was a quick rip through the Home, asking everyone what they knew about it, but the only ones who knew anything at all were the two studious ones who had roomed with Felicity and Bridget, and all they could say for certain was that the RMO's sister and her friend were always talking secretly together, or having quarrels, that something was going on, but they hadn't been allowed by Felicity and Bridget to find out just what. And two of the porters had seen the man who had called hanging around the Nurses' Home since the day the cupboard fell on Felicity, but nothing had been done about him because they had no reason to think he wasn't welcome. After all, he had been invited into the Home to wait in the sitting-room.

Felicity, who had been doing reasonably well after she had come down from theatre, now slipped back and ran a high temperature. Maurice was worried because he couldn't see the reason behind it.

He interviewed Bridget, but she appeared to be quite open and frank and as upset as one would imagine in the circumstances.

"I'm sorry, honestly I am!" she said. "I only told her about that man on the train, the one who came the day the cupboard fell over—but for some reason she got all excited and upset, so I went out, but quick! I couldn't do much else."

"Tell me, in your own words, just what you said to my sister. It's important," Maurice pressed.

"I can't remember word for word. I've got a head like a sieve. I do remember that

252

she asked me to tell her everything, but that's nothing new. We've always pooled our information, especially when one of us got into a scrape."

"And so you told her . . . what?" he insisted.

Bridget fidgeted, but she knew when she was beaten. "Oh, I told her about what happened while the cupboard fell over on her." She glared at Maurice. "All right, it will all come out in the end, so you might as well have it now," and she shrugged elaborately. "It all began when I met a man on the train. Well, what's so terrible about that? I'm tired of boys and this fellow looked—well, no boy, if you see what I mean! Interesting!"

Maurice looked at her with distaste. He really must wean Felicity away from this girl, he told himself. No good would come from such a friendship. With red hair, she must have looked provocative in the extreme. He tried to imagine it. She looked provocative now, even with that mouse-brown shade of hair. There was something about the tilt of her nose, the way she carried her chin out, the very way she wrinkled up her face into a wicked grin when she was scoring off a point—all these things, in Dr. Mann's opinion, simply asked for trouble. Even the shape of the back of her head was cheeky, with that simple boy's haircut, and her eyes slanted too knowingly.

"I expect you've heard a lot about all this," she said, assessing him as she talked. "This chap—"

"Is it asking too much to enquire if you got as far as name terms?"

"His name," she said loftily, "is Claude Langley, and some of my friends know of him, so he can't be so bad," but even as she said it, remembering the scathing way Eileen Shelley had referred to Claude Langley, Bridget kept her fingers crossed behind her back. It was a big lie she had told. Claude was no good and everyone knew it. "Anyway, I could see he wasn't going to be much fun, but unfortunately I'd told him about the Thing I'd borrowed from the glass case at home, and he was very much interested."

Maurice's brows went up. "The Thing? Any use asking for a more explicit description? Don't tell me it was something really valuable from your guardian's collection?"

Bridget couldn't decide whether Dr. Mann already knew the whole story from her guardian or whether he was just being careful to get the facts right now. She decided to be casual. "It was just a tatty old bit of tooled leather or wood or something horrible, and it smelt. It came from some native tribe and some American wanted it. Well, I wasn't going to sell it to any old acquaintance on a train, although I hear from my friends that my guardian believes I've raised some cash on it already. I'm hurt about that. To think such a thing of me!"

"When did you hear about that?" he asked sharply.

"Within the last few hours," Bridget said with dignity. "Anyway, this wretched Claude Langley was mad keen to get the package, but when it came to a game of chase in the guard's van among all the props belonging to some magician chappie who was on the train, I thought I was getting tired of it, so I wrapped up my manicure case in some paper and made sure he saw me doing it, so he had a shot at getting that and I let him and he made off with it. Now, of course, he's mad, and he was trying to contact me to tell me a thing or two about tricking him. He thinks I've still got the Thing! I haven't, honestly!"

"Let's get this straight—you say he made off with it. How? Which station did he get off at?"

"Oh, he didn't," Bridget said airily. She was rather enjoying telling the story now. It really did sound rather interesting, she considered.

Maurice didn't. He got up slowly, his face going brick red. "I think you've been getting at me," he said, in a dangerously quiet voice. "A Thing, a chance acquaintance on a train trying to get it from you, a chase among magician's props, a man jumping the train—! You go too far, Miss Moore, and if you knew me really well, you wouldn't play games. All I asked for was a rational explanation as to why my sister should be so upset after a short visit from you, and what you said to her to upset her."

Bridget's temper didn't show much as a rule, but when it did, it was uncertain. She flared at him now. "It's a rotten shame, disbelieving me when I'm telling the truth. All right, you want to know what I said— well, you can have it, in one wallop. Claude Langley's collecting private details about people, it looks as if he's contemplating blackmail, and your dear friend with no memory (so she says!) is on his list!"

Even Bridget was scared as she saw the way he took that bit of news. She backed nervously away from him. "Well, you did ask me!" she gasped. "It was there, in the newspaper, only I didn't get a chance to read it all, but she'd got her name in the paper and he was interested—"

"Where is this newspaper?" he asked, very quietly indeed.

"In my room," she said. "I'll get it for you!"

"No!" He towered over her, and his rage was a thing to be wary about. She backed slowly to the door. "I'll come with you. We'll collect Home Sister and you can take all three of us to where you've got this man's things, and it's going further than this. You realise that, of course."

Like a little animal, trapped, she stood her ground. Sullenly she said, "I don't care. You can kick people about so much and then they can't take any more. I've got no one. No one wants me. I had a lot of money, but my guardian lost it all. What am I supposed to do? Behave? Work hard for nothing? Be nice to people? That'll be the day! Kick me out—you'll be sorry. I'll see that everyone knows about that Lesley Weldon!"

She turned and ran. He called after her, but she wouldn't stop. Nonplussed, he telephoned through to Home Sister to intercept Bridget, in case she got at that newspaper and destroyed it before he had a chance to see what it said. Home Sister said she would, and that she could see her coming in at the door now.

But Maurice might have saved himself the trouble, for when they went with Bridget to her shared room, there was nothing there. Bridget rummaged in the empty trunk and looked so blank and worried that she couldn't possibly have been acting. "It's gone!" she said, sounding really surprised that anyone should do such a thing to her. "Someone's been here and taken it all, the briefcase too!" After some questioning by Home Sister, and then a visit to Matron, when nothing else could be elicited, Maurice went back to see Felicity.

Something must have been said to Felicity, he thought, as he walked swiftly with eyes downbent, thinking over the whole matter. Something definite about Lesley must have been said to her, to make her lose the headway she had been making, and to collapse in that fashion at the time of Bridget's visit, moreover.

He quietly raged as he walked, to think that Bridget would have the cheek to tell him all that stuff about what had happened on the train! He decided he would have a talk with Matron. Unless he did, it was doubtful if Matron would know really what sort of a girl Bridget was. He was uncomfortably aware that it had been partly his idea that Felicity should have her own friend with her in the training school. If only he had known that his sister would manage to scrape through like that!

It was at that point that he remembered the views of the surgeons only that morning when they had examined her ankle. Poor little brat, after all that effort, only to have to be told—at some comfortably future date, of course—that nursing was out for her. That ankle would always be weak, and a life spent on her feet would be impossible.

He didn't bother to knock on her door, but wrenched it open and was about to walk in, when he pulled up sharply. Alan West was sitting there by the bedside, and Felicity's hands were completely covered in Alan's big ones. They were just staring at each other, with a hunger and a yearning that was too naked to be ignored or misunderstood.

Maurice Mann opened his mouth to expostulate. She was still his baby sister, at varying times the apple of his eye and the thorn in his side, as his grandmother often laughingly told him. Alan West was too old for her, too old to be extracting that heart-tearing look from her, or to be looking at her as if she already belonged to him, his to cherish.

But in that split second, before Maurice had had time to say anything, Sister came softly behind him and touched his arm. He looked sharply round at her, his attention divided, but one look at her told him that the other matter would have to wait. He pulled the door to, and turned to her.

"What is it, Sister?"

"There's an emergency on, sir. A man, found in the shrubbery, just outside the Nurses' Home. The man who visited your sister's friend recently, the day of her accident."

"What did you say?" he gasped.

"Yes, it's a bad business, sir. They seem to think he fell off the flat roof."

10

GENERATIONS of girls in the Nurses' Home had used that flat roof for illicit comings and goings and not sustained a scratch in the process, yet Claude Langley lay unconscious, and not likely to recover.

Everyone was discussing it. "What can you expect?" the irreverent young ones said among themselves. "He's past climbing about! Honestly, I thought he was Moore's uncle! Funny girl, isn't she? She doesn't seem a bit upset!"

"Well, not upset on his account, perhaps," Ann Taylor said thoughtfully. She knew Bridget rather better than the others because as a PTS girl with a perpetual headache she had been worried more than the others by her new roommate. Bridget's giggling and chattering, her noisy banging about and her total lack of consideration for others hadn't impressed Ann in Bridget's favour. "Upset about his visit rather than for him because of his accident, if you see what I mean. I just wonder what he was doing there."

"Yes, that's just it! No one saw him come in, but he must have come in the front door, which is the only way he knew, after the fiasco of a visit he had, the day the cupboard fell over. Funny business, that was, don't you think? Poor old Mann, catching it like that! They say she won't be able to walk again."

"Get it right, you clot, or you'll have the RMO after your blood! She won't be able to walk again on the wards, which is rather different! Whoever heard of anyone not walking about again after a busted ankle? Be your age! But ward work—well, my feet are killing me, all the time, morning till night. I don't wonder she won't be able to do it, and if you want my private opinion, she won't be sorry. All right, she scraped through PTS. So what? I can't see her getting through the later exams."

Bridget listened to all this, from the seclusion of the store-room at the end, where tea was made when anyone felt energetic enough, but the fashion had changed lately and cocoa was the vogue, made in the tiny kitchen on the floor below. The store-room was deserted and she used it to get away from everyone else's questions.

Outside the store-room window was an old safe, unused since the previous orderly had left. The present woman in charge of that floor was scandalised at the thought of keeping anything in the safe, so it was deserted and Bridget had used it as a temporary hideout for the briefcase and the newspaper concerning the girl with amnesia. He had broken into the Home, she fretted, but he must have been disturbed trying to find her or her room (one or the other) and tried to escape by the flat roof.

She wondered what she ought to do now. All her life she had wriggled out of things rather than face the music. That had been Felicity's habit, facing the music for both of them. And now Felicity was too ill to do that. Bridget must make up her own mind, and it wasn't so easy, now that she had done that marvellous bit of acting and convinced everyone that the things had been taken out of her trunk. That had been an instinctive piece of work; mostly because she wasn't going to be blamed for anything, but also because she wasn't going to let Dr. Mann have the satisfaction of learning the truth about his precious Lesley. But how long could the thing be allowed to run on?

Because she knew what was in that newspaper account, Bridget was uncomfortably aware that the private eye her guardian was employing would also inevitably stumble on to the truth about Lesley. She thought about it, and decided that it couldn't do her any harm, unless they pressed her to say what scandal she thought was unearthed by Claude Langley. How did she stand, then? Claude Langley would regain consciousness and talk, in all probability, because hospitals had police sitting by the bedside of suspected persons, ready to take down a statement, didn't they? And supposing Claude Langley felt ill enough to think he was going to die, and decided to make a clean breast of everything? What then?

Irritably she gave up the problem and went out. She ran into Toby Fairbairn, in whites, tennis racquet and net of balls well in evidence. "Want a game?" he asked doubtfully. Bridget appeared to have gone off him rather, lately, and he couldn't understand why. They had been such friends.

Bridget gave it thought and finally agreed. They went to the courts, secluded from the hospital windows, hemmed in by trees; a nice place on a summer's day. No one else was patronising the courts, for once, and Toby was happy. But even Toby's happiness could be shattered.

Bridget's game, like everything else about her—her work, her friendships, her pleasures—had a passing brilliance. No reliability whatever. One day she would be breathtakingly good, another day (as today) indifferent in the extreme. Her manner was indifferent, her game indifferent. Toby gave up in exasperation.

"What's the matter with you, Bridgie?" he exclaimed. "Here we are, with a marvellous fine day, the courts to ourselves and time on our hands, and you play the most awful game I've ever seen you play! Something on your mind?"

She joined him and considered him. Considered whether it was worth confiding in him. He was a nice young man, but so far he hadn't impressed his personality on her enough for her to be even aware (when he wasn't with her) of what he looked like. Now she took in every detail, perhaps for the first time. His was one of those faces that was filled with blazing honesty rather than good looks. His nose was lumpy and his jawline not very strong; his lashes, brows and hair were of that pallid brown that is so difficult to describe, but his eyes, very bright blue, were the steadiest and the kindest she had ever seen. For perhaps the first time in her life she found herself recognising kindness being offered to her, unreserved, uncritical kindness, and it took her by surprise. She didn't know how to handle it. She was desperately afraid of appearing weak, silly, all the things she despised, yet she wanted his kindness and common sense and friendship so much. That wasn't like her, either, she reflected. She, who had always snapped her fingers at people, and forged ahead alone, must be softening up, and that was bad.

"Come on, I can see there's something on your mind—something more, that is, than the usual trouble. Unload, girl! I've got the time and I'm a good listener. You know that!"

He was, too. She said, "Let's go out somewhere. Somewhere where they won't find us."

"What for?" he asked blankly.

"Oh, do you have to have reasons for everything?" she raged at him. "Well, if you want to know, I'm about to be kicked out of the hospital and I've been told to wait in the Home until sent for, so that seems a good excuse for just not waiting, but for going out and pleasing myself."

"No. No sense in that," he said, shaking

his head. "Besides, it's not polite, and there's nothing more shabby than the person who really likes being rude to everyone else just for the fun of it."

"Then why be friends with me if you don't like what I'm like? You won't change me, so don't try, Toby!"

"I don't want to change you, Bridgie. I like you as you are. I know what you're like—a little girl who's trying to be all adult and experienced and worldly wise, and she thinks the way to show people she's like that is to cock a snook at them and push and be rude. But you're not like that really. I think you don't really know what you're like, and to play safe, you tell yourself you're not very nice. Not giving yourself a chance, is it?"

She glared at him.

"Well, let's go and sit on one of those benches in the sunshine and be matey and have a talk, why don't we? As I see it, Bridgie, you've been trying to think things out and you've made things look blacker than they are. You ought to tell someone all about it, you really ought, because then you might find that the other person's opinion is that things aren't as black as they seem. Try me!"

"All right," she said, glowering ahead of her, at the courts bathed in sunshine, the masses of trees, the smooth green turf beyond and, like a kindly guardian, the red brick mass of the hospital, the windows all a-twinkle in the bright light, brooding comfortably over everything. "For a start, I think I'm sickening for something, because having made a mess of everything and being for the high jump, I find I don't want to go. What about that?"

"I wouldn't want to go, either," he told her.

"Why not?" she asked suspiciously.

"Well, it's not a bad place to live and work in. A bit like one big happy family really. I know we have our ups and downs here, but who doesn't? On the whole the living's comfy, the grub's good, and the social scene isn't all that bad. If I can get my game of tennis and work I like with people who aren't so bad really, well, that's it, then. Isn't it?"

271

He wasn't much good with words and explainings and he knew it, but he was doing his best. She stared, unconvinced.

"Take me, for instance," he went on, persevering. "There's only my uncle, at home. He doesn't think I'm so hot, if you know what I mean. Well, can't say I blame him. I inherited quite a bit of money, see, and he naturally thought I'd go into his firm with him, taking the money with me. He could do with it—I know that. But I had other ideas. It's my money. And I didn't want to work with him in his beastly firm. I wanted to do this," and he waved an expressive hand towards the hospital.

"Why?" Bridget asked suspiciously.

"I dunno. I just wanted to. My uncle didn't understand that either, and it's no use—I can't explain. I just like my work, and I like being here, and that's the way it's going to be."

"For always?"

"I wouldn't say for always. Who knows what might turn up? That's the jolly thing about life, not knowing what's round the corner. Oh, it may not all be honey. I grant you that. It might be blooming awful. You have to take the rough with the smooth. I find if you just take a deep breath, and just keep jogging along, you get through the toughest patch eventually, and there's usually something not half bad, when you do get through. See what I mean?"

"That might be your idea, but I wonder what you'd feel like if you were in my shoes," she remarked. "For a start, I had quite a lot of investments which my guardian now tells me have flopped, so I've got to work, and all I can do is to have the most appalling bad luck and get kicked out."

"Bad luck about the money, but after all, what's money?" he said. "I've heard a few rumours about what you did, but I don't believe them all," he told her very seriously. "How would it be if you were to take your time and give me your version? You owe it to yourself, you know."

She decided she would. She frowned in concentration and told him about the interview with her guardian over the investments and how upset she had been, and of how she had gone on the spree, but found the young man missing, so in defiance of everyone she had stayed on the train and let a comparative stranger scrape an acquaintance. Toby didn't interrupt, and he earned full marks for that. She was amazed. Until today she hadn't really considered him out of a crowd—he was just one of many young men at the hospital, good enough for general escort duty. Now he suddenly stood out, and forced her to see him as he really was: a young man with no good looks or gift of oratory, who could yet talk her out of a bad mood, and persuade her to regain her lost self-confidence. A young man with a personality to be reckoned with, who took and kept her attention for some time (no mean thing, with the elusive Bridget!) and who presumed in his quiet way to give her advice and contradict her in her wild statements. He had suddenly sprung to life and it made her uneasy. No young man had done quite what he had done this afternoon.

"I told the RMO a frightful yarn," she admitted. "Well, I told him the truth about what happened on the train and he wouldn't believe it and thought I was having him on, so I lost my temper and told him a lot of wild nonsense about someone breaking in and taking the things from my room, and sure enough he believed all that, when I'd got them hidden all the time."

"Oh, lordy, you shouldn't have done that to the RMO. He'll be cross," said Toby.

It was hardly the word to describe Maurice Mann's simmering, uncannily quiet rage, Bridget felt, but she didn't say so. She said instead, "Well, now you've heard all about it, you surely can't keep on saying you understand and that my chances of surviving this row aren't so bad! Well, I just don't know what to do!"

"How about letting on what was in the newspaper about that nice girl the RMO's so keen on?" suggested Toby.

She was a little put out because there was no smile any more in those nice eyes of his; he looked very grave. He made her feel she'd been really wicked this time, instead of merely inventive and courageous, which was what she had persuaded herself to believe.

"Well, if you're too scared to tell me, take me to where it is, and let me read it. You'd better, if it was so bad as to interest a chap like that, who'd rake over all the dirt in people's lives and use it."

"That's what's so funny," Bridget exploded. "I know I told Felicity it was awful, but she ought to know me by now. It wasn't awful. That was just it. When you think of the other things in the other newspapers he was carrying, it wasn't like that at all."

He studied her in silence. She burst out, "It's no good looking at me like that! It's all gone too far now to put right! It's no good showing you the newspaper because you'll only get involved with me in all this, and I've done enough one way and another, even to you. Well, pinching you from Felicity—"

"You didn't pinch me from Felicity,"

he said quietly. "I liked Felicity. It had nothing to do with her being the RMO's sister, either. I just liked her. She's a nice girl. But that's all. I didn't want to marry her, and she didn't want to marry me."

"How do you know? Did you ask her?" Bridget retorted.

"No need. It doesn't need half an eye to see she's batty over Dr. West, and it doesn't need a lot of brain power to discover he's completely potty over her. Besides, there's someone else I like a whole lot more, though I shall be laying up a store of trouble for myself in the future, that's if she'll have me, which I doubt." And he put his hand half shyly, half firmly, over Bridget's.

At any other time she would have thrown it off, but at this moment it gave her such a warm comfortable feeling that she let it rest there. She looked away to where a sparrow was having a dust bath, and reflected how happy some people seemed to be able to be. Even the daft birds could slop around in the dust, and look as if they hadn't a care in the world.

"What exactly are you thinking about, if it's me you're referring to? I mean, you'll be taking on a load of trouble into the bargain. You don't know what my school record was like, or what sort of friends I have, or what my guardian thinks of me. He thinks he hasn't managed to teach me what's mine and what's not."

"Well, he hasn't, has he, love?" Toby said gently. "As to the Thing, as you call it, how would it be if you tried very hard to make me understand just what it is and where it might be at this moment?"

She hooted with sudden derisive laughter. "I couldn't do either of those things! Don't be silly! The last time I saw it, it was tucked between the back and the seat on that train, and I, like the miserable worm I am, suggested to Felicity that the Lesley person might have pinched it."

"Well, it's done and can't be undone. Never mind that now, and if you're going to bawl, I wish you'd do it elsewhere. That sort of thing doesn't impress me. I find it tiresome. Now come on, love, this Thing of yours. First of all, you say you took it from its glass case?"

"Borrowed it," she amended. "To make my guardian wild—and wasn't he just that?" and she looked gleeful suddenly at the memory, and sniffed and mopped her wet face.

"Oh, dear, love, you'll have to grow up, won't you?" Toby said sadly. "Well, and as you didn't have to bust the case, presumably it had been left unlocked, so he can't blame you entirely. Now how big was it? Show me."

When she did, he got out a typed letter, and turned it over to its clean back and began to sketch a rough shape with a pencil. "Like so," he murmured. "Colour? Dirty brownish-green or black. Looked old." All this he wrote down. "Now, what was it made of? Wood or leather or bone? Like any of them! All right, I'll note that down. And the pattern you say was on it—can you give me some idea of what that was like?"

She did her best and he scribbled industriously. "And you wouldn't know where your guardian got it, I suppose," Toby murmured. "It's taking shape and looks vaguely familiar, but I'm sure I don't see how—"

"Of course I know where he got it!" she said impatiently. "It came back in his things from his last trip in Central Africa, oh, years ago, from some ghastly little tribe whose name sounded something like Wa-Jo-Jaw or something. He was always talking about it when I was a child. Drove me up the wall. Honestly, he's got all sorts of hideous trophies in that room. I hate them. They're like a lot of the tatty old stuff you see in museums. He got this thing from the chief for saving his life (so my guardian said, though I don't have to believe it!) and then he wants to sell it to this American just because he was offered thousands of dollars!"

"Wait, this rings a bell," Toby said worriedly. "There was a chap I was at medical school with, who came from those parts, and he used to tell me about the tooled work that was kept as treasures in the tribes. I suppose your giddy little head couldn't take into account the fact that if a thing is frightfully old and hand-made and riddled with history and people have died to preserve it—"

"Ugh! Don't! You're giving me the shivers."

"You're giving me the shivers when I think of how casually you make off with something that might be regarded by some people as of priceless worth, just because there isn't another one like it. And you stuff it in a seat—oh, really, Bridgie love, what am I going to do with you?"

"Never mind the Thing! What do I do about owning up to the RMO for having fibbed about the newspaper? And do I let him see it because it's about his girl-friend? And what happens if Claude Langley spills the beans?"

"I honestly don't think there's a chance of that," Toby told her seriously.

"I don't understand," Bridget said uneasily.

"It's only the impression I got, mind. I haven't been near the chap. He's not my pigeon. But from what I've gathered, they don't really expect him to 'do', you know."

"Oh, this daft hospital jargon! What do you mean? That he won't recover consciousness?" Bridget gasped. "But how could that be? He only fell off the flat roof!"

"Girls who are used to climbing in and out, when breaking bounds, and who have youth and lissom limbs through PT and sports, are not likely to damage themselves as a gentleman in his early forties might do, who never did a day's exercise in his life, I should think, and who probably fell flat and struck his head on something hard as he arrived," Toby murmured, getting up.

Bridget got up, staring blankly. "Where are we going?"

"To get the trophies a man is about to lose his life trying to retain?" Toby asked softly. "We have to show them to someone who will know their importance to that chap." But as Bridget mutinously shook her head to that idea, he said, "Well then, I suggest you go and ask nicely for permission to go and visit your friend Felicity and make your peace with her. And then perhaps later you'll think again about the newspaper article, at least, because it might mean an awful lot to the RMO and that poor girl who has lost her memory. She really has amnesia, you know," he added, with an understanding smile.

11

FELICITY didn't particularly want to see Bridget just then. She had been lying there serenely re-living the visit from Alan West.

She hadn't quite known what to do when he had taken her by surprise and presented himself. He stood there, slightly amused, slightly abashed—a curious mixture for him—and his arms were full of a gigantic spray of florist's blooms tastefully arranged, a precarious bundle of glossy magazines which threatened to escape his hold at any minute, a cellophane-wrapped gilt basket of fruit and a box of chocolates, the ribbon bow of which dangled absurdly from one finger.

"I'm not much good at visiting patients and I never know what to bring, so I settled for the lot," he said, dumping them on the table by her bed. "How are we?"

"You want the strict surgical details

which I pestered until I received? Or just a general remark to the effect that the patient is as well as can be expected?"

"Oh, chirpy, aren't we? Good! I was afraid you'd bawl or something. I get embarrassed easily. Is my neck red?"

That made Felicity giggle and he grinned appreciatively. Sobering suddenly, however, he said in a queer low tone, "Joking apart, what happened? Truly! No holds barred, no protecting best friends—just the bald truth. I want it, *stat* —tell you why, afterwards."

Their glances met and locked. Suddenly it was all different. Not just Alan West looking down from his height of years and inches and importance and experience, but the man who could make her all queer and uneasy and fluttery and excited and walking-on-air sort of happy. She wanted to cry, but she was exhilarated too, and it worried her, because she knew she would do anything he said. Even to telling on Bridget; because Alan and all he stood for now mattered much more than silly, selfish, shallow Bridget, who had no kindness in her and wouldn't know what loyalty to a girl-friend meant.

"It was a ruse to get that man out of the room while his briefcase was switched, only the plan went wrong. I didn't get my foot out of the way in time before the cupboard fell, on account of slipping on the polished floor."

As Maurice had, so Alan looked thundery when Bridget was mentioned, and filled with rage at her stupid ideas and pranks. "So you had to be the scapegoat," he said savagely.

"All the luck of the game, darling," Felicity shrugged. "It might have been Bridget getting caught switching the briefcases, or she might have tripped in getting away. Only it was me."

He forgot that Felicity indiscriminately and flippantly used the word 'darling', and he thought she was using it as an unconscious endearment. "What do you think I feel when I hear you're in this predicament?" he said roughly.

"Irritated?" she hazarded. "The nice RMO's daft young sister. Oh, don't think

I don't know! Don't think I haven't heard what people say. One day when I thought I was doing particularly well with my work, I was prancing along past some open windows, when I heard a man's voice say, 'Remember Dr. Mann? Nice chap. Go far one day.' The other fellow with him said, 'What, Mann of the Medical Wing? Yes, I remember him!' And the first one said, 'You won't believe this, but that's his young sister!' Stunned silence followed. I was cut down to size all right! I agree, poor old Maurice, what a rotten burden for such a super doctor, but I didn't ask to be here, did I? I didn't ask to be me!"

"Shut up, Felicity," Alan said softly, and unexpectedly he took her hand, and with a curiously half awkward, half desperate gesture, he put it to his lips and held it there. His eyes met hers, and before the look in them, her own fell away. "Never mind what people say," he told her in a very low tone. "You're all right. Well, *I* think so, anyway. But you know that, don't you? You must do. Ever since

I first saw you, you've been . . . under my skin. Look at me, Felicity."

He had forced her to look at him, taken her chin in his hand and turned her scarlet face to his. "Do you like me at all?" he had asked abruptly.

And she had nodded and said, "Yes, terribly," and he had kissed her. A long kiss that sapped her energy but tossed her to the skies in sheer elation.

And now here was Bridget, looking determined, just when Felicity wanted to be alone to think about Alan and to remember what he had said about her not being able to train to be a nurse because her ankle would always be weak, but it wouldn't matter because he wouldn't want his wife to be on the wards, anyway, although he firmly believed she would have made a good nurse. Sweet, sweet words to someone like Felicity, who had tried so hard, so belatedly.

Bridget said, "Toby Fairbairn made me come and tell you *all*," and she proceeded to do so, with energy and thoroughness. But although Felicity was surprised to learn a lot of things she hadn't known before about it, it somehow no longer mattered.

"And that's not everything. I like Toby, and if he asks me, which I still can't believe he will but he says he will, then I shall say yes, because I'm fed up with racketing around on my own. Only I pinched him from you."

"No, you didn't. Besides, there's someone else." Felicity said it dreamily. Bridget stared at her.

"Alan West? Toby said so, but I didn't believe it—you mean it? Crikey! He's old! Oh, well, congrats!"

She stayed another half an hour, talking feverishly. When she went, Felicity felt drained of energy, and flinched a little when her brother looked in, with Lesley.

Lesley smiled warmly. "Hello! Not to worry, we're not stopping. Want anything?"

Felicity shook her head. "No, thanks. Got everything." I've got Alan West's love, her thoughts sang. What more do I want in the whole blissful, wide world?

Maurice said, "We just came in to say hallo. Lesley's pretty fed up, so I'm taking her to the pictures."

"What's on?" Felicity asked with a polite show of interest, but it was clear to them both that she didn't really care. She had her own thoughts to think.

"Haven't a clue. We'll look in on the way back," Maurice said, patted her hand affectionately, and went out.

"She's in love," Lesley said softly. "Is it that nice Dr. West, d'you suppose?"

"Why, yes, I suppose it would be!" Maurice said in surprise. "So that was why he was looking so anxious just now when he stopped me. Started to say he had something important to discuss with me, and then he got called away."

"Do you mind, Maurice?" Lesley murmured.

His hand briefly held hers, tightly, as he handed her into his car. His eyes caressed her. "No, of course I don't," he said shortly. "Those who can get some happiness, let them, I say!"

He had hoped the film might be a

290

comedy. Anything to make her laugh. But it was a spy thriller. Events which neither of them could follow chased across the screen. Lovers clung briefly and were torn apart by State police, guns came out from cracks in curtains, and people fell dead. Maurice looked comically at Lesley, and said, "What did I pick this show for? Would you like to go out?"

She pulled a face, and began to gather her things together. She had dropped a glove and they grovelled on the floor to find it, bumping their heads together. With smothered laughter they came up for air, but meantime the film had moved its locale apace. Now the main characters were swaying on a train. The camera moved from the inside of the train to the outside, showing it swinging round curves on a track up a mountain. Lesley's face assumed a mask of horror.

"It's a fake shot," Maurice said hastily. "Don't look—let's go!"

"No, it's not that," she gasped, and she couldn't tear her eyes away. Someone on the train was looking out at the end carriages which came clearly into view as the train rounded the bend. Briefly, before it straightened, the train's last coach was all visible and something fell out of a window. Something thrown, relevant to the story, Maurice thought, but Lesley suddenly crumpled and fell at his feet in a dead faint.

When she came to, they were in a little room with a big first-aid cupboard and a couch, and two or three people milled about trying to be useful, to Maurice's directions.

Lesley struggled up, ducked her head down between her knees briefly, and then sat up. "All right now," she said, and smiled at the people. "It's all right, don't fuss me—I'm a nurse. I should be ashamed, behaving like this!"

Then she saw Maurice. "Hello," she said. "What are *you* doing here?"

Maurice stood up. "Would you leave us? She'll be all right now, but we have things to say to each other."

The manager and the other people left them, and Maurice sat down facing her again. She looked very ill, sitting there with her head in her hands, arms resting on the small table. "Why am I here?" she murmured.

"Now you just take it easy," he told her firmly. "Let it all ride. Give yourself a chance," and he kept his hands in his pockets because he wanted so badly to sweep her into his arms and kiss her and make her memory go to sleep again. Torn two ways, the lover didn't want her to remember, though the doctor in him did.

"That film just now . . . the train . . . oh, heavens, how am I going to bear it?" she moaned, and covered her eyes.

"You said you were a nurse," he reminded her, and unconsciously he became just the doctor, sitting ready to give advice and help, cool, impersonal. "Nurse . . . who?"

She was shaking all over. "Garth. Lesley Garth. I trained at St. Antony's in Mortonhill."

"Mortonhill?" he said sharply. "So near?"

She nodded. "I left for William's home

—Dr. Weldon, that is." Now she was just repeating the tumbled thoughts as they came into her mind, her voice flat, her face drained of colour and emotion. "Dr. Weldon was to be my—"

"*To be?*" Maurice repeated, hardly able to believe his ears. "You mean, you *weren't* married to him? But the label on your case said Mrs. Lesley Weldon," he prompted her, very gently. "That was why we all called you Lesley Weldon."

She shook her head, frowning. "No, we didn't get married."

He thought of the private detective. "So that was why no record of the wedding could be traced," he murmured.

She hardly noticed. "We were all ready. William got held up. Emergency. It made us late leaving the hospital. My best friend was worried and thought she'd help by labelling everything with my new name. William didn't like it—said it was unlucky to do that. But people do—"

"People do," Maurice agreed. "What happened then?"

"We were on the train," she began, and

then she broke down. It was some time before she could continue. "I didn't see it happen. I was told afterwards. He fell to his death, trying to stop a man who was going to jump from the train."

"Oh, my dear!" Maurice groaned, and took her hands in his. In his desire to help her, he forgot his fears that she would look at him as if he were a repugnant stranger. She turned to him, and there was no question of dislike in her eyes. She turned to him as the one person left in the world.

"Maurice, I don't know what happened then. I stayed somewhere up north, for a time, and then I came south again, with the idea, I suppose, of going back to my own hospital at Mortonhill. Whether to be with my friends or just to collect my things, I'm not sure. Only we didn't get as far as Mortonhill. It was so horrible, what happened on that train." She turned dark, stormy eyes up to him. "A man fell out, just as the train came round a bend, just like on that film just now."

He comforted her as best he could, but it wasn't really private there. As soon as she had recovered a little, he took her to a quiet, good restaurant, and made her eat a little food, and drink some brandy. She didn't like it, but agreed that it would be the best. Her old life was taking over; she was no longer shy, uncertain Lesley, but a confident Lesley who had been a fully trained nurse, very much impatient with herself for being the patient.

"I ought to have known," Maurice said. "You said, when you first went into a ward bed, that you wanted to put a student nurse right when she was fiddling with the drip stand. That should have told me. Why didn't it?"

She smiled at him. Tremulously. "Why, why? What a horrible frustrating little word it is. Why did I lug that case about with me, with my trousseau in it? I couldn't touch it, either to use the things or to alter the labels, but I couldn't bring myself to leave it anywhere. I just walked around with it, clinging to it." And still remembering, she forced herself to say, "The man, who fell from the train—?"

"I've been thinking about that, too. I've

heard a slightly different story, from Bridget Moore, who was on the train with you. She is (or was, rather) a friend of my young sister Felicity. She was going to join my sister who was training as a nurse at our hospital."

"I do remember that," she said, her eyes still troubled. "I do remember that girl on the train—no, wait, she had red hair, didn't she?"

"It gets changed," he said dryly. "It was blonde next, and now it's brown. You won't know her."

"I might, at that. She bothered me, I remember, rather like a fly. She was fidgeting with something she was pushing under the upholstery—but the man who fell! What were you going to say about him?"

"He didn't fall. He jumped, because, I suspect, he thought he had taken from Bridget the thing she had been hiding in the seat. It was, so I understand, something with a rather high value set on it, from an antique dealer's point of view!"

Slow horror dawned on her face. "Oh, no!" she whispered.

"What is it?" He took her hand across the table. "Drink some more brandy!"

"No, no more of that stuff. Oh, Maurice, this is awful. It's all coming back to me. Listen, she left her case behind, so I hopped off the train to find a porter to give it to, and then—I must have fainted, I think."

"You did," he said. "And now I've heard all that happened, I'm hardly surprised. The shock of your fiancé's death and then seeing something that might have been a repetition of it—terrible thing to happen to anyone!" He gently reminded her of all that had happened since.

She sat nodding, listening, fitting it all into place. Then she said, "Oh, Maurice, this is all rather awful! You see, it has a new significance now. At the time, all I wanted to do was to make myself remember, even though I shrank from the things that might come back. You see, when I was first put to bed in the sick bay of the Nurses' Home, I was bothered by that handbag. It wasn't mine. I knew that instinctively. There was nothing personal in that handbag."

"Whose could it have been, do you suppose?"

"It belonged to one of the nurses at my old hospital," she said, smiling at the memory. "She lent it to me because my own, a rather splendid new one, had got packed by mistake. Too many cooks, and we were so pushed for time." Her face clouded again. "She lent me her spare bag just for the journey. Anyway, to get back to what I was telling you—I went on searching (I'd been left alone to get undressed) and I found some things in the pockets of the suit jacket. I ought to have told someone, but you see, it was a terrifying experience not knowing who I was or anything. I might have been, or done, something I would want to hide. Who knows? There was *something* awful my mind wouldn't let me remember. I was quite sure of that!"

"What did you find?" he asked her.

She shrugged. "Parts of someone's letter, arranging a meeting. It sounded shady. I felt it might be mine, but I hadn't a pen to try out my own handwriting."

"Where is it now?"

"The bit of the letter and the list? Oh, still in the pocket of the suit. I ought to have done something about it, but so much has happened since, and I've been scared about what might be found. There was the other thing . . ."

"What other thing?"

"It's coming back to me. I was curious about what that girl had hidden. She was being rather pestered by that tall man . . . yes, the one I saw the other day when I was having a meal out with you, remember? If it wasn't him, it was very like him."

"It was him. Tell you later how I know."

"Well," Lesley continued, "I put my hand in and drew out a very strange thing, a piece of handcraft, I should think, with an Eastern or African suggestion about it. There were big patch pockets in that suit, so I put it in, meaning to slip it to the girl when she got away from that man. I couldn't leave it there on the train. Then I remember thinking it might have been stolen and left for someone to pick up. I had enough on my mind and I didn't know what to do. Maurice, I have to tell you I was looking at it in that bed, when they sedated me, and I've never seen it since."

"Don't worry. It'll all be put right, I'm sure. It was something that girl borrowed from her guardian who has brought a lot of such stuff home from the Middle East. That piece came from Africa and he had a buyer for it, but that's his problem and hers. Meantime, about that man . . ." and he told her what had happened to him.

"Now I suggest you stop worrying about everything and rest, my dear. This is a big day."

She nodded. "I shall keep on remembering things, I suppose, but the thing is, what do I do now? I've got a job at the hospital, haven't I?"

And as time went on, that all came back to her. "Do you want to keep it, stay with us for a while," he said, rather diffidently, "or would you care to consider my plan?" His eyes searched hers. "We did feel we meant something to each other, didn't we?"

He was aware of his heart beating so madly he felt he was choking. Would she remember all the sweet moments they had spent together, and the one time he had kissed her?

"That was a helpless person with an aura of mystery around her, who called herself Lesley Weldon and leaned heavily on poor Dr. Mann," she said, with a wry smile. "I'm no helpless, clinging female, my dear. I'm a nurse and I love (well, I used to love) my work. I would want to go back to it, I think. How about waiting till you see me on the wards, and see if you like me as much, as I used to be?"

"If you want breathing space, my dear, you must have it. But it won't make any difference to me. You're the one for me. You have been since I went to meet Bridget at the station, and you collapsed in my arms. Nothing can change the way I feel about you. You're still you."

"I have to wait a little, to be sure," she said, rather breathlessly. "Please, Maurice."

Later he telephoned Matron to tell her what had happened. Matron had her own news to give him, so he let her talk first.

"Your young sister's friend—Bridget— has been to me and made a complete confession," she said, and she still sounded surprised. "She brought with her the briefcase that had belonged to Mr. Langley. There's a very large part of a newspaper article there, which is about your Mrs. Weldon, Dr. Mann."

She waited. She sounded a little odd, he thought. "Yes, Matron, what does it say?" he forced himself to ask.

"It's a very tragic story and explains a lot," she said. "It appears that the poor young woman was a nurse engaged to a doctor in her hospital, who was killed falling out of a train trying to save a patient."

"Yes, and what else, Matron?"

"That is the gist of the story, except to chat about their lives. They were well-known locally, and well-liked, it seems. But the odd part about it was that Miss Moore who didn't read it all or very carefully, thought that it contained an item of scandal which Mr. Langley proposed to use, but when I myself carefully scanned the newspaper, I found a marked item, clearly of possible interest to such a man, and of no connection at all to our amnesia patient."

Maurice felt rather light-headed with relief. Not that he had had any doubts, but it had worried him why that man should have had an article about Lesley in the first place. "Oh, Matron, thank you!" he gasped. "And now I must tell you a few pieces of news! First, our amnesia patient has recovered her memory. It's been quite a shattering experience, frankly," and he told her very briefly, because Matron had little patience for a lot of description, what had occurred.

"Well, I'm more glad than I can say, Dr. Mann. It does seem as if everything is clearing itself up nicely, don't you think?"

"I hope so. Might I enquire what is to

become of my sister's friend? I don't want Felicity upset, you understand."

"Indeed I do, and partly for that reason, and partly because it appears that Dr. Fairbairn has a proprietorial interest in Miss Moore which might be a very good thing for her, she is being allowed to stay, with reservations."

"Reservations?" and there was a smile in his voice.

"At the moment she is on punishment duty—cleaning out the sick bay in the Nurses' Home."

Bridget was not, however, being so usefully employed at that moment, and it was as well for her that Matron couldn't see her, wild-eyed, clutching something with wet hands and staggering down to the floor below to use the forbidden telephone in Home Sister's Office. She rang Toby.

"Is that you, Bridgie? Listen, love, you just get off this line and finish your punishment duty before you stop for chit-chat or you'll really be for the high jump!" he said.

"Toby, will you listen? I was on my

knees cleaning the floor and minding my own business when the most peculiar thing happened. You remember the Thing, the one I borrowed from the guardian and lost on the train? Well, I found it up there in the sick bay! I really did! Am I going mad?"

"Bridgie love, take it easy!"

"But what's it doing here, of all places?"

"Are you sure it's the same one? There aren't two?"

"No, absolutely not! Besides, it even *smells* the same. Kind of fusty, and *old*. It's a horrible thing! I bet the tribe used it for ju-ju rites or something nasty."

Toby thought a moment. "Where exactly did you find it?"

"I was cleaning the floor and something was sticking out of a gap between the floor and the wainscot. I knocked it out, thinking it was an old bit of wood, but it wasn't. It really *was* the Thing! I bet I know how it got there—those lazy maids just mopped under the bed and sent it skimming and it stuck in the gap where the floor's dropped."

Toby made up his mind. "Put that phone down, love, and stay where you are, and keep hold of that treasure, while I belt over and find Home Sister. This is too big for us to handle! We've got to have help!"

"Yes, but don't you *see*?" Bridget insisted. "The only way it could have got here was through that Lesley Weldon. *She* was in the bed near where I found it. I've just remembered that!"

"Now you be careful, love, what you say about her!" Toby warned, but Bridget wouldn't listen.

"Well, it's true! It must be! Look, she was sitting near where I hid it on the train. She must have had it in bed examining it and fell asleep or something, and it must have fallen off the bed." She swallowed. "I don't care if the RMO *is* batty over her —that Lesley Weldon's a thief!"

There was a gasp, Home Sister's voice in the background and the receiver crashed down on its cradle.

The rest of that day was a hectic one for Bridget, her guardian and his private eye, hastily summoned to the hospital, and for

Toby, who was determined to make the Colonel's acquaintance and let him know that there was at least one person who saw a lot of good in the now disgraced Bridget. Felicity and Alan were involved, too, with their part in the affair, and Maurice and Lesley. All of them, with Matron and Home Sister and the Medical Superintendent, were all so concerned with sorting out the result of Bridget's confession and final discovery of the Colonel's lost property that the news of Claude Langley's slipping away from his precarious hold on life was in the nature of an anti-climax.

The grapevine fairly hummed with gossip; the women in Maurice's medical wing loved the news of a romance and there was more than one here, but the medical staff talked more about Claude Langley.

As Maurice said to Lesley, some days later, "I really don't think I've ever felt like this about a patient before. I always hate losing them, but that poor chap would have never been any good, you realise that? You know the kind of injury he had? You saw the notes, I believe."

"Yes," she sighed. "Still, it's a life, although what would have happened? He was wanted by the police, wasn't he? And poor Colonel Partridge—the publicity—"

"No one says 'poor Bridget', I notice," Maurice said, with a grim smile. "Yet Fairbairn is as pleased as punch with getting the Colonel's permission to take that girl off his hands as soon as is decently possible."

Lesley chuckled. "She'll be different when she's married to him. She clearly adores him, even if she doesn't know it yet. And your Felicity is making strides now you've assured her she can marry that nice Dr. West as soon as she likes."

"Yes," said Maurice, turning her round to face him. "And that reminds me. All these people about to enter into a state of future bliss—what about us? I'm sure it would be good for both of us to get married as soon as possible. I never did believe in breathing-space. Besides, someone else might come along and convince you that he was a better man for you than I would be."

Lesley shook her head. "No. There's not a man breathing who could do that. Not even my poor William. He was a dear, but . . . Oh, Maurice, can't you see, dearest? You're the only man for me!"

THE END

Books by Anne Durham
in the Linford Romance Library:

NEW DOCTOR AT NORTHMOOR
MANN OF THE MEDICAL WING

Other titles in the
Linford Romance Library:

ISLAND FIESTA
by Jane Corrie

Corinne found herself trapped into marrying Juan Martel. He expected her to behave as a docile Spanish wife, and turn a blind eye to his affairs. How on earth could Corinne cope with this mess?

THE CORNISH HEARTH
by Isobel Chace

Anna was not pleased when she ran into Piran Trethowyn again. She had no desire to further her acquaintance with such an insulting and overbearing character.

NOW WITH HIS LOVE
by Hilda Nickson

Juliet hoped that Switzerland would help her to get over her broken engagement, but all that happened was that she fell in love with Richard Thornton, who was not interested in her.

LAND OF TOMORROW
by Mons Daveson
Nicola was going back to the little house on the coast near Brisbane. Would her future also contain Drew Huntley? He was certainly part of her present, whether she wanted him to be or not.

THE MAN AT KAMBALA
by Kay Thorpe
Sara lived with her father at Kambala in Kenya and was accustomed to do as she pleased. She certainly didn't think much of Steve York who came to take charge in her father's absence.

ALLURE OF LOVE
by Honor Vincent
Nerida Bayne took a winter sports holiday in Norway. After a case of mistaken identity, entanglements and heartache followed, but at last Nerida finds happiness.

THE WAYWARD HEART
by Eileen Barry

Disaster-prone Katherine's nickname was "Kate Calamity". She was a good natured girl, but her boss went too far with an outrageous proposal, because of her latest disaster, she could not refuse.

FOUR WEEKS IN WINTER
by Jane Donnelly

Tessa wasn't looking forward to going back to her old home town and meeting Paul Mellor again—she had made a fool of herself over him once before. But was Orme Jared's solution to her problem likely to be the right one?

SURGERY BY THE SEA
by Sheila Douglas

Medical student Meg hadn't really wanted to leave London and her boyfriend to go and work with a G.P. on the Welsh coast for the summer, although the job had its compensations. But Owen Roberts was certainly not one of them!